C000070270

THANKS FOR LAST NIGHT

A GUYS WHO GOT AWAY NOVEL

LAUREN BLAKELY

LITTLE DOG PRESS

Copyright © 2020 by Lauren Blakely

Cover Design by Helen Williams.

All rights reserved. Without limiting the rights under copyright reserved above, no part of this publication may be reproduced, stored in or introduced into a retrieval system, or transmitted, in any form, or by any means (electronic, mechanical, photocopying, recording, or otherwise) without the prior written permission of both the copyright owner and the above publisher of this book. This contemporary romance is a work of fiction. Names, characters, places, brands, media, and incidents are either the product of the author's imagination or are used fictitiously. The author acknowledges the trademarked status and trademark owners of various products referenced in this work of fiction, which have been used without permission. The publication/use of these trademarks is not authorized, associated with, or sponsored by the trademark owners. This book is licensed for your personal use only. This book may not be re-sold or given away to other people. If you would like to share this book with another person, please purchase an additional copy for each person you share it with, especially if you enjoy sexy romance novels with alpha males. If you are reading this book and did not purchase it, or it was not purchased for your use only, then you should return it and purchase your own copy. Thank you for respecting the author's work.

ALSO BY LAUREN BLAKELY

Big Rock Series

Big Rock

Mister O

Well Hung

Full Package

Joy Ride

Hard Wood

The Guys Who Got Away Series

Dear Sexy Ex-Boyfriend

The What If Guy

Thanks For Last Night

The Gift Series

The Engagement Gift

The Virgin Gift

The Decadent Gift

One Night Only: An After Dark Novella

The Heartbreakers Series

Once Upon a Real Good Time

Once Upon a Sure Thing

Once Upon a Wild Fling

Boyfriend Material

Asking For a Friend

Sex and Other Shiny Objects

One Night Stand-In

Lucky In Love Series

Best Laid Plans

The Feel Good Factor

Nobody Does It Better

Unzipped

Always Satisfied Series

Satisfaction Guaranteed

Instant Gratification

Overnight Service

Never Have I Ever

Special Delivery

The Sexy Suit Series

Lucky Suit

Birthday Suit

From Paris With Love

Wanderlust

Part-Time Lover

One Love Series

The Sexy One

The Jewel Series

A two-book sexy contemporary romance series

The Sapphire Affair

The Sapphire Heist

ABOUT

A sexy new friends-to-lovers standalone!
Let me list the reasons why dating the sexy, charming
pro hockey star is a bad idea:
1. He's one of my closest friends
2. All our friends are friends
3. The wounds I've got from past relationships go deep.
And so do his.

We're both devoutly single -- it's just safer for the heart
that way. But there's no reason *not* to bid on the
gorgeous, clever athlete at the charity auction this
weekend. If I win, it'll be a "friendsdate."
And I do win.
I win him big.
And hard.
And all night long.

The trouble is . . . what happens in the morning?

Thanks For Last Night is a standalone romance in The Guy Who Got Away series. The other titles are Dear Sexy Ex-Boyfriend and The What If Guy.

THANKS FOR LAST NIGHT

By Lauren Blakely

Want to be the first to learn of sales, new releases, preorders and special freebies? Sign up for my VIP mailing list here!

HER PROLOGUE

Teagan

Experts tell women some crazy shit.

Like this gem—when you hit twenty-nine in New York City, the creep sets in.

The dating creep.

Sounds like a catchall category for all the jerks and jackholes women learn to avoid, and if you haven't yet, do yourself a favor—they are never worth it.

But no. When lifestyle gurus say "dating creep," they mean your dating prospects will—supposedly—slow to a molasses-speed trickle. If you listen to these experts, you should just box up your stilettos and take up your knitting needles.

Sure, twenty-nine is still technically young. But it's only one year from—shudder—*thirty*. And in Manhattan, where there is an influx of perky college grads flooding the streets every freaking June, the big three-oh is a deal-breaker for some dudes.

So, chop-chop. Get moving, ladies.

The only glance you'll get from guys in bars is on their way to checking out that pretty young public relations strategist next to you, or the quirky-cute book editrix and her friends, all less than a quarter-century old.

The only solution is to lock a man down while you can!

Because soon, you can forget the idea of an adorable, glasses-sporting hottie chatting you up while you're reading travel guides in a cozy indie bookstore in the cutest meet-cute of all, maybe one where you drop a stack of papers and he picks them up, while casting love eyes at you. That is an under-thirty-only scenario.

Are you scared yet? Desperate and ready to settle for less than love?

Don't be.

Don't buy into the madness, ladies.

I'm rapidly approaching thirty-three, and I say, bring it on, *calendar*. I'm not afraid of birthdays, nor am I afraid of being alone.

I like my own company.

I'm *that* woman. The woman in the red dress, strolling down Lexington Avenue, AirPods blasting pop music, pink handbag swinging sassily from her arm—because where else would a lady carry her mace?—without a care in the world.

Maybe that's not a daily event, but it's the single-in-the-city montage unfurling under the opening credits in the romantic comedy flick of my life. It would have a kick-ass girl-power soundtrack too.

And as for the closing shot? No spoilers here, because there are zero guarantees that more than one person will be riding off into the sunset. Because I refuse to accept a Hollywood Ending requires romance.

I'm living proof.

I'm the happiest kitty in the borough of Manhattan, and I don't need a man on the reg to enjoy the catnip of life.

Catnip tastes fabulous when you're single.

Even if a smidge more Tinder swipes go left instead of right now that I walk on the—gasp—dark side of thirty.

But I don't let this evaporation in the dating pool bother me, because those men don't know what they're missing.

I'm the woman who knows how to have a good time.

I don't mean like *that*—wink, wink—though I do, also, mean like *that*.

Mostly, I mean *this*—I like fun and games. I like going out. I like trying the smorgasbord of things this fabulous city has to offer.

So, if and when the dating creep kicks in, I'll do what I usually do.

Say "No, thanks," and walk on by.

But here's what dating experts *don't* tell you.

You'll have to fend off your friends the most when you're over thirty.

Once they all fall ass-over-elbow in love, they will have zero self-control when it comes to their new favorite hobby—matchmaking.

Once attached, everyone becomes a cupid.

They want everyone to be as happy as they are, and they can't resist aiming their arrows at your heart—yours and those of whatever single guys they know.

Lately, my coupled-up friends have a particular target in mind and are champing at the bit to pair me up with him.

Ransom North.

Stud hockey player. Dry sense of humor. Laid-back attitude.

We're the holdouts. The last single people in our group, so natch, we should get together—the happy-go-lucky social media strategist and the chill NHL all-star.

Maybe in a parallel universe, we might have been a good fit. It would certainly be convenient for our circle of friends—until it wasn't.

In *this* world, that's the issue when it comes to Ransom and me.

My friends *are* my family.

I don't want to take a chance of ruining the *only* family I have by messing around with someone who joins us for brunch, Ping-Pong, paintball, laser tag, and so on.

It's best to keep Ransom at an ogle-distance and out of reach, thank you very much.

At least that's what I tell myself.

Until the night I told myself the craziest lie of all—

that I could get him out of my system and return to the way things were.

But it won't work.

After Ransom, I'm going to need a whole new normal.

HIS PROLOGUE

Ransom

Some guys believe in mottos.

Plenty of women do too.

People plaster their world with their life's catch-phrase—stick it on their walls, print it on their mugs, ink it on their bodies.

I'm not one of those—the motto plasterers. I don't have posters in my pad or ink on my skin, and all my mugs come from my little sister, who chooses only the snarkiest of sarcastic slogans.

But I am definitely a mantra guy.

I've got mine stored nice and handy up here in my head, accessible at a moment's notice.

Most are pretty basic—respect your family, put down the toilet seat if you live with a woman, and play your motherfucking heart out every time you hit the ice.

My list of dos and don'ts is longer, but if I hit the two biggies—*don't* be a douchebag and *do* be more chill—I pat myself on the back and feel pretty damn good about myself.

That's how I lived in my twenties, and those guidelines are why I have the life I want now at thirty. They've never let me down.

Except once.

That one time they failed me.

So now my number one, never forget, always follow is this: *Fool me once, shame on you. Fool me twice, shame on me.*

When you've allowed yourself to be tricked so cruelly, once you know the sharp, stabbing pain of naivete so deep that it hollows out your heart—you learn your boundaries.

The ones you won't cross again.

I found my line the hard way, and now I know better.

Love sucks, so save yourself a world of hurt and avoid it at all costs.

Especially if the woman is a friend.

Case closed.

Except I have a sinking feeling I'm about to get fooled again.

So, put that on a mug and drink up.

1

RANSOM

She rounds the corner, just a blur of silky red hair, fleet feet, and a kamikaze heart.

Her white-and-orange pistol swings slowly as she hunts me.

From my hiding spot behind a dimly lit doorway, I narrow my gaze, take aim, and fire off a punishing round of green lasers at the lithe redhead. "You're going down, King!"

I strike a fatal blast to her chest. Teagan goes all-in on the drama, letting her pistol clatter to the floor as she collapses to her knees.

Sputtering, she clutches her heart and coughs like she's performing Shakespeare, going for the save. Rules are rules, and our mutual friend Bryn devised them for today's game of laser tag—if you can make your killer laugh while you're dying in the last round of the battle royale, you can earn another life.

When it comes to sports, I don't believe in do-overs or mulligans. But sportsmanship also means respecting the rules of the game as they're laid out, even the silly ones. So my job here is to remain impervious to Teagan's dramatics, implacable as she twists and writhes, contorting her face and making sounds reminiscent of a cat heaving up a hairball.

Ice.

I'm the North Pole, just like I am in the rink.

Nothing breaks me, and nothing breaks me down.

Though if something were to chip away at my armor, it might be gorgeous-as-anything Teagan King flopping onto her back, looking like a break-dancer doing the worm while being electrocuted.

Oh, hell.

She's so ridiculous fake-dying that the seed of a chuckle takes root in me.

A kernel of a laugh sprouts and gathers strength in the center of my rib cage, gaining speed now.

Then she rises like the undead, reaching out her arms and groaning like a . . . sexy zombie.

How the fuck is that possible?

Zombies are not sexy, but my laugh grows faster, climbs higher, until it takes over my chest, gripping me in a quick convulsion.

Dammit.

Maybe the hot auburn-haired zombie didn't notice.

But she sits up completely, points at me, and grins in epic satisfaction. "You laughed, North. Admit it, or forever be known as Laser Tag Liar."

I clench my jaw, wanting to deny it. But I won't do that. The gods of sports hate cheaters more than they hate commissioners and all-star games.

I give in with a long, frustrated groan. "Fine. I'll admit it. I laughed for maybe one nanosecond. But only because you're such a drama queen, King."

"Come on, North. Admit it was funny."

"Fine. It was a little funny, you going all undead."

She pops up and shimmies her sexy hips. "Wait till you see my vampire. That'll lead me to victory too."

"You haven't won yet, cocky vampire."

She flips her hair off her shoulder in a sassy little move that I can't look away from, because . . . that hair, that face, and most of all, *that confidence.* "Oh, but I will. Now, get your ass back out there, North, so I can take you down. Because I'm the only one who can."

There is some truth to that.

The woman is a sick competitor, with a fearless heart and a ferocious appetite for victory. She makes the most of her second life in the arena, darting, dodging, and firing at me relentlessly.

We go mano a mano for ten, close to fifteen minutes. And in this final shoot-out, her team against mine, there are no mulligans. It's a fight to the finish, ducking down hallways, turning through tunnels. As I prowl around a dark corner, searching for my nemesis, she steps out from the shadows, aiming straight at my heart.

Cold. Ruthless. Determined.

She fires.

I'm dead. Just dead. Game over.

I curse, but fair is fair.

"Good job, killer." I drop my gun and offer her a hand, since that's what you do when you win or when you lose.

"I humbly accept your courteous adoration," she says in her most gracious voice as we shake.

I roll my eyes. "I wouldn't really say it was adoration."

"Now, now. We both know it was."

"I'll let you have your delusion," I say as we pick up our pistols and return them to the check-in counter. I gesture to the bar adjacent to the arena. "Want to join the crew, King?"

"Let's do it," she says, and I sweep my hand out for her to go first.

Because I'm a gentleman—and a wise gentleman always seizes the chance to enjoy the rear view.

Teagan's ass is just so damn yummy, and I'm an ass man.

Wait. Nope. That's not entirely fair to her breasts, which I very much enjoy checking out too. But asses are easier to ogle. So I do that for a few seconds as she exits the game area. I do it knowing the ogling will go nowhere. Knowing, too, that she's got so much more going on than a delicious form. I enjoy her company too, so I don't feel guilty about enjoying the sights when I can.

Some of our friends are waiting for us outside the arena. With a victory dance, Teagan smacks palms with her laser-tag teammates—first with my good buddy Logan, then with Bryn, Teagan's bestie and the reason we're celebrating here today. Bryn recently opened her own consulting firm. She's signed deals with a few marquee clients, so today's laser-tag-plus-karaoke-plus-beer is on Logan as we toast to his woman's career success.

"You brought it home for our team, girl. So proud of you," Bryn tells Teagan.

"I'm all about teamwork. And beating Ransom," she says.

Bryn smiles, sporting the happy look that Logan seems to put on her face constantly. Logan and Bryn met a year ago and are kind of ridiculously in love.

Which, come to think of it, is how I'd describe all my good buds these days. Logan, Oliver, and Fitz—all with hearts in their eyes, dopey grins on their mugs, life partners by their sides.

Logan pats Teagan on the shoulder. "I, for one, am glad you took down this competitive bastard." He deals me a satisfied smirk. "Ransom has tried to destroy me in Ping-Pong far too many times, so I'm stoked someone can pummel him in laser tag."

I snort-laugh. "You deserve to be pummeled in Ping-Pong, Logan."

"Why? Why do I deserve it?" Logan fires back.

"Everyone who plays me deserves it," I say as we head into the bar. "I don't hold back in any game. Balls to the wall is the only way to play. If you can't handle the heat I bring with a paddle, you need to get away from the Ping-Pong-table fire."

Teagan cuts in, laughing. "You do know that sounds racy on ten million levels, Ransom? From the balls to the heat to the paddle."

I wiggle my brow. "That's what she said."

She parks her hands on her hips. "Way to steal my punch line."

"Guess I just beat you to it." I set up the opening for her favorite zinger. Until very recently, the woman has dropped in *that's what she said* with such gleeful abandon that it should be her nickname. Or it could, if it weren't such a—*ahem*—mouthful.

That, and she's made a resolution to stop saying her catchphrase, claiming it was going to get her in trouble at work. It's been a blast trying to trip her up, but she's a tough one to crack.

Like now, when she shoots me a saucy grin and resists with a shake of her head. "I'm not going to touch that one with a ten-foot pole."

"Are you sure?" I say, egging her on. "A ten-foot pole might be fun—with the right person."

"You two and your innuendos," Bryn puts in. "Grab a table while we snag some beer, okay?"

"Will do," I say as the lovebirds go place our orders.

Teagan and I snag a high top, while a familiar voice fills the bar with a mostly in-tune warble. On the low stage by the karaoke setup, my teammate Fitz belts out "The Time of My Life" in a duet with Summer, Logan's twin sister.

Huh.

They're not too shabby, but still deserve ribbing.

"Way to go, Kenny and Dolly," I shout.

"Donny and Marie have nothing on you two," Teagan seconds. Leaning toward me, she echoes my thoughts too, saying, "They're not half bad."

"Yeah, I know. Hidden talent, maybe?"

"I'm convinced everyone has one," she says, and there's some truth to that. I suppose we all have something we're good at.

We watch them for a little longer. Fitz pretends he's singing the love song to Summer, but he keeps making eyes at his fiancé, Dean, who moved here from London last year. Dean's a few tables away with his friend Leo, laughing. It's some kind of private joke, I'm guessing, since Dean and Fitz have plenty of those.

Good for them. They're also ridiculously in love. All around me, every-damn-where, my band of brothers is toppling. Single soldiers have become fallen warriors, losing their minds to the siren call of love, leaving me the last man standing.

Well, I've already been there, done that, have the battle scars to prove it. I have no desire to repeat the experience.

But having fun? Bring it on. Light and easy? That fits with one of the top-tier items on my do-and-don't list. *Do* be more chill.

"Best karaoke duet ever?" I toss the question to Teagan, staying on the train I like to travel with her.

She stares at the ceiling, brow furrowed, lips pursed. "'Endless Love' is pretty good."

"For the cheese factor, right?"

"Of course. So much cheese, you could make a sandwich."

"'Endless Love' is pure cheddar. But 'Islands in the Stream' is a classic duet too. A little schmaltzy, but easy for mere mortals to sing."

She nods, eagerly agreeing. "Unlike, say, 'Shallow.' Why do people even attempt to duet that song?"

I hold up stop-sign palms. "Don't look at me. I would never attempt to follow Gaga and Cooper."

"Those are some words to live by." She snaps her fingers, eyes lighting up. "I've got it! 'Summer Nights.' That's the best karaoke duet ever."

I sing, ask her to "tell me more, tell me more," and she shimmies her shoulders, providing the harmony.

"We're a good duo," she says. "Maybe that's our hidden talent."

I narrow my eyes. "Don't think you can trick me into being your teammate. You and I—we are competitors. And I still have a laser-tag score to settle with you."

"Good luck with that."

When the tune ends, Summer and Fitz leave the stage, Summer going to join her husband, Oliver, who's chatting with Dean, while Fitz makes a beeline for our table, pointing at me, eyes furious. "I heard the news. You choked in the arena," Fitz says, shaking his head in disappointment. "You brought our team down."

I shoot him a *what gives* look. "Dude, you were eliminated in the first round today. You've been out here singing 'Electric Avenue' for the last thirty minutes."

He fires off an indignant look. "I did not sing 'Electric Avenue.' I would never sing 'Electric Avenue.'"

"Guys, stop mentioning 'Electric Avenue,'" Teagan chimes in, covering her ears for a second. "You're going to give me an earworm."

"Exactly," I say to Fitz. "Now you'll have T's earworm on your conscience, along with how you did nothing for our team. I was the *only* reason we lasted that long."

Teagan hums, tapping her lip-glossed mouth, which is distracting, I admit. Hell, the way her finger presses to her lips is a double whammy. Now I'm thinking of lips and fingertips.

"I don't know," Teagan says, giving me a naughty look. "That's not what I heard about how long you last, Ransom."

I dole out a sharp stare. "I have excellent stamina."

An eyebrow arch is her answer, and then she throws a saucy question at me. "Do you though?"

"Don't make me prove it to you," I say, as if I don't want her to take me up on that.

Wait. I don't. I swear, I don't.

Brain, remember your mantras: Love sucks, and friends with breasts do not get to be friendly with your body.

Fitz raises both hands like he's about to take off. "Well, I think that's my cue to make myself scarce."

Teagan pats the table. "Don't be silly. Stay, Fitz. We always talk like pigs."

"I am very proper," I say, all hoity-toity. But I say to my bud, a little hurt in my voice, "Also, I can't believe you're hounding me for not winning laser tag, which is more than I can say for either of our sorry asses on the ice a few weeks ago. That second round of the playoffs was brutal." I shake my head sadly.

"Low blow, Ransom," Fitz says. "It's devastating to come so close, but not close enough." But the truth is, he's not terribly sad that we missed out on the Stanley Cup Finals. All his postseason energy is on his guy. Fitz is marrying Dean next weekend, and he's pretty much the happiest man I know.

As for me? Not making the finals definitely still stings. But days like this and time with friends make the loss hurt a little less. I'm hoping the ache disappears completely before the charity gala this coming weekend. I have a bet with some of my frenemies who play for the Yankees that our hockey team will beat their fundraising total, and I intend to do my part to decimate the Bronx Bombers, because that's what we do—that's how we are. Because my teammates don't back down from a dare—especially one with our charities benefiting from the competition.

Logan and Bryn return with beers, so we toast to Bryn's new business. After a long pull, Teagan tenses, then reaches into her back pocket. Grabbing her phone, she slides her thumb across the screen, peering at it closely. She looks up apologetically. "Email from a board member. I know it's after hours, but . . ."

Bryn shoos her away. "Answer it. I know it's important."

Teagan rises. "I'll do it in the hall, so I can focus." She pats my shoulder, squeezing it, and says to the crew, "Don't let Ransom sing 'Summer Nights' without me, or I will make him sing 'The Boy Is Mine' with me instead."

I should fire off a quip or a snarky reply, but when my eyes drift to her hand on my shoulder, I'm kind of transfixed by her touch. What would it feel like if she wrapped that hand a little tighter? Maybe roped that other one up into my hair?

Mmm. Yeah, that'd feel fantastic.

Or hey, how about I do that to her?

Whoa.

Hold on.

Where the hell is my brain galloping to?

That's *hell no* territory.

I blink away my wild thoughts. "Your threats don't scare me, King," I say, serving up the trash talk. "I'm secure enough in my manhood to sing 'The Boy Is Mine.'"

"Fine. Then you and I will need to lay down some karaoke bets when I return from the ladies' room." She sashays away, and I watch her as she goes. The whole ensemble—snug jeans, pink Chuck Taylors, a light-blue tank top—is doing things to my head. Add in the spring in her step and the flip of her hair, and they're activating all kinds of neural pathways.

Ones that had definitely been buzzing before but seem to be crackling faster and stronger today.

Maybe because of how she looks in that shirt? Or maybe it's her lips? But then, her hair is invitingly lush too.

Hell, she's just insanely attractive. As in, one of the hottest women I've ever seen in my entire life. And that's saying something, because my life has never lacked for attractive women. I've enjoyed an embarrassment of riches in that department.

Lucky me.

Trouble is . . . Teagan is a friend and only a friend. We run in all the same circles. Teagan and I are too tangled up in each other's lives.

In short—our friends are our team, and you don't bang a teammate.

I shuck off thoughts of Teagan in bed, something I do so frequently these days I could earn an Olympic medal in it.

But I could use some practice being subtle, judging from the wide-eyed, knowing way that Fitz, Logan, and Bryn are staring at me when I return my gaze to them.

I take a guilty gulp of my beer, like I've been caught with my hand in the liquor cabinet. "What?" It comes out more defensive than it should.

Bryn gestures in Teagan's direction, a *duh* look in her green eyes. "We need to talk about that."

"About what?" I ask, playing dumb.

Fitz taps the table. "About the way you stare at Teagan."

Busted.

"I was thinking of strategies to defeat her next time in laser tag," I lie.

Bryn snorts. Logan cackles. Fitz rolls his eyes, then says, "Listen, man. It's time for an intervention."

"An intervention for what?"

"To help a brother out," Fitz says. "Sometimes a man needs a kick in the pants. Consider this your kick. You and Teagan should go out."

"I have to agree with him. You're two peas in a pod," Logan seconds.

Bryn nods excitedly. "Yes. You guys practically finish each other's sentences."

"And," Fitz says emphatically, leveling a serious gaze at me, "she'd be good for you."

I tense at those words—*good for you*. I know what Fitz is getting at, but he's treading on dangerous territory. If he so much as mentions my ex, I will shut down. I don't need to hear her name. Not ever again. Fitz *only* knows about her because I finally served up the whole sorry story to him a few months ago when I needed to get it off my chest, unraveling the pathetic tale of the way she pulverized me when I asked her to marry me.

Then I said, *Let us never speak of her again.*

So I slam that door and take a simpler way out. "Look, Teagan's great, but I don't mix pleasure with friendships. And we're all friends, so . . ."

Undeterred, Bryn wiggles her brows. "And you're also both fun. You should have fun . . . with each other." She steeples her fingers, takes a beat, and draws a preparatory breath. "So, here's my idea."

Bryn lays out a plan, a simple one, where as soon as she says it, the potential is obvious—potential benefits and potential amusement. Some of my favorite hobbies include besting my buddies and giving away money. Her plan involves both.

And damn, it's brilliant.

So brilliant it kind of pisses me off that I didn't think of it first.

But I didn't, so I give Bryn deserved props.

"That's kind of genius," I say.

"You just need to get Teagan on board," she adds.

Fortunately, convincing people is one of my *unhidden* talents, so I've already got some ideas. "I can do that."

Fitz's eyes twinkle with mischief. "And I guess

you've realized that, this way, you could potentially beat the fundraising pants off the Yankees, the Knicks, and the Giants, and nab that grand prize award at the gala. Because we all know how competitive you are."

I nod in acknowledgment. "The most competitive."

Bright red hair snags my gaze as Teagan returns to the bar.

It's game time, and I need to go set up a play.

2

TEAGAN

Here's the thing New York City has done to my generation.

It's made us connoisseurs of quirky Sunday Funday events and propagated them to every day and night of the week.

Fancy midnight mini-golf? You'll find it in Manhattan.

Jonesing to make your own cheese? Why not make some wine with it too? You can definitely do both in Brooklyn.

You can even have a party where you make mittens, cover them in glitter, then compete to eat as many cupcakes as you can while wearing your new mittens. Head to Queens for that messy fiesta.

The city is a mélange of millennial activities. Some are eye-roll inducing, but they're not all pointless. We have all experienced our fair share of shit in our lifetime —some more than others—so sooner or later, we desperately need some fun to drown out the drumbeat of bad news.

An oddball outlet for stress has become necessary for mental health.

Including mine.

That means, tonight, we don't stop at laser tag.

We can continue the celebration of Bryn's awesomeness at karaoke or choose darts or shuffleboard instead.

In the hallway, I tap out a quick reply to Nancy Fenester, one of the trustees who approves all my requests for fundraising, to let her know I'll have a list for the third quarter soon. That sent, I tuck my phone back into my pocket and return to the bar, ready for our next activity.

Ransom is solo at the table. The hockey hottie tips his forehead to the dartboard.

"Favor of my choice if I beat you at darts," he says, sliding right back into our competitive banter.

That's how we are.

At the glitter-mitten party, we bet on who could make the most garish mittens. I won. At mini golf, we threw down greenbacks over who'd make the most holes in two. He nailed that odd victory.

But this wager has me curious and then some. Because a favor is a brand-new currency.

"A favor? What kind? As Sandy and Danny would say, *tell me more*."

"It's a good favor. One you'll like," he says, a little teasing in his tone.

"Tell me more *now*, then," I say, pointing to the floor in a demanding gesture.

He shakes his head. "Only if I win."

I shoot him an *I'm not crazy* look. "I'm not signing up for a favor if I don't know what kind."

He gives me flirty eyes. The gold flecks in his hazel irises twinkle with Ransom mischief.

Wait. Is he hitting on me? He can't possibly mean sexual favors. Can he?

My traitorous body wouldn't mind him laying one of *those* on me. Or two of those.

Or maybe stop counting and just go *all night long.*

After all, Ransom's frame defines "chiseled," and his face is the prime example of masterfully carved. His warm eyes probably grace the Wikipedia page for "soul-searing." He's the most tempting possible temptation the goddess of temptation could have placed in my path.

But there's that little matter of how he's never shown a bit of romantic interest in me.

Isn't this a skeezy way of making a move though? Because . . . ew. "This isn't, like, some *Indecent Proposal* thing, is it?"

He blinks, then flinches as the dots connect. "What? No. Are you kidding me? Fuck no."

Okay. While I didn't want him to be propositioning me, I didn't want him to recoil at the idea either. "Fair enough."

"Because that's tacky, Teagan." His tone has shifted to earnest, his gaze intent, and his use of my first name underscores that the clarification is important to him. "I'm not going to bet you for sex, because that's fucking disrespectful. I have sisters. I was raised to treat women right."

And . . . I'm going to pretend I totally never thought he would proposition me. Especially since I'm not supposed to picture the horizontal mambo with him anyway. I punch his shoulder and keep a lighthearted tone. "I know. I was only teasing." And hell, that was super convincing, even to my ears. I expect an Oscar to come my way soon.

"Good," he says, then resumes our usual bantering. "Anyway, you'll like this favor."

I arch a skeptical brow. "How can you know that if you won't tell me what it is?"

"Because if *you* know, then it's no fun. And you like fun." His expression says *Am I right, or am I so right?*

Damn him.

Because he is both those things. "True, but I don't want to commit to darning your stinky, unwashed-for-weeks socks."

He pulls a *what do you take me for* face as we make our way to the dartboard in the corner of the bar. "Please. I have a laundry service. I'd never ask for a favor that lame. And to ease your mind, why don't you tell me some of your off-limits favors?"

I tap my chin, exhaling deeply. "For starters, I won't mow your lawn."

"Totally understandable." He lowers his voice to a stage whisper. "Also, since I live in the Village, I don't have a lawn."

"How convenient." I snag several darts from a table, and he takes some too. I point one at him. "Here's another favor on my no-go list. I won't grab a mattress on the street that says 'free' and help you drag it into your apartment."

He sets a hand on his heart. "I promise I will never ever ask you to haul any nasty, disgusting, bedbug-infested object from the curb into my home."

I go full Alexis from *Schitt's Creek*, making a cute little *aww* sound, then tap-dance my fingers up his chest. "You are, like, the sweetest guy ever."

His eyes drop to my hand on his pecs. For a few seconds, his gaze seems to match mine. There's a tiny flare of heat in it, but then it disappears so quickly I think I've imagined it.

I yank my hand away like I can erase that minuscule touch.

He clears his throat. "Continue. What are your other favor deal-breakers?"

"I won't be your Scrabble partner. I know that's hipness sacrilege when retro board games are the height of cool, but Scrabble bores me."

"Ouch. Does that apply to Words with Friends too?"

"Obviously. Both suck."

He exhales forlornly. "As a Words with Friends lover, that line in the sand hurts. But I'll take it on the chin. And I'll offer you this final proviso too. If you don't like the favor once I tell you, you can trade it in for a karaoke song of *my* choice."

"So I have nothing to lose except being subjected to Rush's 'Tom Sawyer'? Earworm of all earworms. All right. I'll accept your wager." I offer a hand for shaking.

He takes it. "Smart woman. But that is *not* my favorite song."

I smirk. "I guess we'll never know what your favorite is, since I'm going to crush this game." I give a playful shimmy of my hips as I flash him a *let's do this* smile.

Treating Ransom like I would one of the other guys makes it easier to deal with that cocky grin, those see-inside-me eyes, and that sculpted-by-the-NHL body.

Ransom is a pal is a pal is a pal.

With our wager in place, I take aim with a dart and let it fly toward the board. I wince in frustration when it barely grazes the outer ring, the sharp point stabbing the edge.

"You know the goal is that bull's-eye in the middle, right?" Ransom asks dryly.

"Gee, thanks. Appreciate the tip."

"I'm helpful like that." He takes his turn, firing a dart straight down the line and notching it squarely in the center.

He smirks.

After a whistle of appreciation, I say, "That was beautiful, and I hate you."

I fire the next dart. It scrapes the edge of the board and falls listlessly to the floor with a sad thump.

"Oh, bummer for you," Ransom says, not bummed in the least.

I roll my eyes and pick up the little weapon. "There is still time for me to stage a comeback."

We fire away a few more rounds until he easily wins the game, then I cross my arms and tap my toe. "Fine. You won. I guess I'll have to take you shopping for your sister's birthday, since I bet you detest shopping. That's the favor, right?"

Laughing, he shakes his head. "I don't hate shopping. And that's not the favor."

"We'll hit the boutiques tomorrow morning at nine just for fun, then." I wiggle my fingers. "For now, tell me what you want."

He licks his lips, drags a hand through that thick, dark hair I bet is as soft as a silky cat's, then exhales like he's prepping to dig down deep. "Do you happen to know anyone who's a sucker for animal charities and who also maybe likes to help people too?"

"Hey. Don't call me a sucker," I say, but I'm smiling because he knows there is only one answer to his question. I do know someone. I *am* that someone.

"My bad. Wrong word." He pats his chest. "Someone who's a total pushover like me."

"You're forgiven. And yes, I might know someone who fits the bill."

"Good. Because I have a charitable proposition for you."

"Don't keep me in suspense." I'm jazzed now, excited in a whole new way. This is my passion—I work to give.

Because I don't have to work.

Which, on paper, sounds awesome. But, in reality, the reasons for it hurt like hell.

"The annual player's charity auction is this weekend," he explains. "The one for all the sports teams in New York."

That piques my interest. I'd followed the auction last year on Twitter because the pics set my social media feed aflame. Well, they *were* of hot athletes in suits and tuxes. Who doesn't need a fire extinguisher with all the sparks lit by that imagery? "The one where players pick different causes and compete to raise money for them?"

"Yup. So, all sorts of organizations benefit. Wounded Warriors, first responders, recycling programs, animal rescues, and, of course, my personal favorite— companion dogs," he says.

I smile. "I didn't know that was your favorite." I'm curious why, but don't want to get sidetracked when I'm dying to know what he's getting at and where my favor comes in.

"So, in addition to the event funding some great causes, I've got a little bet going with some of the Yankees. Whichever team brings in the most for their charity, the other has to match the total donation to the winner's organization." The opening beats of "Love Shack" float over the bar from the stage. Sounds like Oliver singing. "That's some serious extra incentive to come out on top," Ransom says.

"If it means more money for charity, I'm not going to knock any weirdly competitive bets among friends."

"Frenemies," he corrects.

I arch a brow. "Sounds more like you're friends who compete with each other, but sure, I'll call you frenemies if you want me to," I say playfully. "Especially since we're talking about matching donations, which are awesome, generally. Even better if they stoke your competitive spirit."

"Yeah, it doesn't take much to fan those flames."

"This all sounds amazing," I say, but I furrow my brow because I'm not sure where I fit in this scenario, though I think I can make a good guess.

I give away a lot of money from my parents' foundation to worthy causes. This year, I'm aiming to hit a certain number, and as long as the board of trustees—led by Nancy—approves my donations, I'm close to the mark. I'm assuming Ransom wants me to pony up. Since the causes he rattled off are ones the board usually signs off on, I suspect it'll be an easy yes. "So, you want me to make a matching donation too?"

He gives me *that* smile. The one he knows how to fling in a woman's direction to get her to say yes. The one that's both warm and sexy at the same time, all curved lips and a hint of a dimple—as if his polished looks, fiery humor, and calendar-worthy physique weren't devastating enough.

Just add in a dimple to make him irresistible. That's fair.

"Sort of," he answers. When he glances down, a tiny bit shy, a flop of dark hair brushes his forehead. He runs a hand through it, pushing it back. What a lucky hand. "But I was actually hoping you'd want to bid on me in the player's auction."

I stare at him as the "Love Shack" refrain from the stage echoes in our corner of the bar.

Did he just say what I think he said?

Glitter on the highway indeed.

"Bid on *you*?" I point at the hunk in front of me, making sure I understand the scope of this favor. "In the auction with the players from all the pro teams?"

"Yes. I'll cover the cost," he adds.

Ah, that makes more sense.

This *is* a business deal.

And that's just fine. Completely, totally fine.

I squash that tiny smidge of hope wishing for more because I don't want more, I don't want more, I don't want more.

"What do you have in mind?"

A smile and shrug come my way. "I'm going for the big kahuna. The player's auction draws the most attention, the biggest donations. If you bid on me, I can make sure I go for the amount I want to give away, know what I mean?"

Ah. The light illuminates the whole room. "You want to rig the auction?"

He volleys me another grin, one that says *But it's cool because it's more money for charity.* "Yes, but I'm giving it all away, and it's my money, so who cares if I'm running up the number?"

Raising my hands, I shake my head. "Not me. I don't care that you're running up the number. It's pretty clever actually, enlisting a partner in crime."

"Thank you." His winning smile spreads wider. "We'll make arrangements in advance. The amount. How high to go. But yeah, I want to win for many reasons. One, because I want to raise the most. And two, bragging rights with my frenemies."

I sketch air quotes. "Your 'frenemies.' Of course."

He laughs. "I swear they're frenemies, not friends."

"It's a fine line. But in any case, you came to the right cohort. I'm totally cool being Brad and George lining up a little flimflam." If he wants to go all *Ocean's Eleven*, recruiting his team of one to pull off a caper for charity, I'm game.

With *his* money.

A beautiful reverse heist to make sure he gives away the most.

"What could go wrong?" he asks.

"Nothing," I say with a bright, legitimate smile. This sounds like a hell of a good time. But my brain hangs on a detail. "What about the prize I'd be bidding on though? The date with you. Would you forego that?"

An unexpected coil of tension winds tightly through my body as I wait for his answer. I want to cross my fingers, since I'm hoping—really hoping—that he says no, he wouldn't want to skip it.

Which is dumb. Because I can't date him.

I just want to know the score.

He scratches his jaw. "Well, considering it's the Win a Date with a Player auction, and the teams' PR people post publicity photos, yeah, the prize would be . . . a real date. So we'd go on a real date, presumably. Dinner, dancing, a carriage ride."

I pretend to retch.

He cracks up. "Yes, I know you hate carriage rides."

"Because I love horses, and I don't believe for a second they want to pull carriages in the park. Maybe we could go for a trail ride instead."

"Consider it done, pardner," he says, all cowboy and southern sexy.

"So," he continues, rocking back and forth on the balls of his feet. He seems oddly nervous. Nerves aren't something I associate with Ransom North, so I'm not sure what to make of them. "What do you say?"

Our friends have been trying to smash our faces together for months, and we've resisted like magnets.

Yet, if I bid enough, we'll go on that date they've wanted after all.

But it's not a face-smashing date.

It's a date for a cause.

Lingering lust for the man aside, it's a date that could help me achieve my goals.

I'd be honoring my father's final wishes.

Helping to promote the value of giving.

I can do that with a picture that'd spread a thousand words.

As a social media strategist for a dating and relationship site, I know how powerful photos on social media can be. Shots from a charity event like this, with a sports star of his stature, can absolutely raise awareness for a good cause.

That's what I vowed to do with my parents' money.

That's what I want more than anything.

To keep up their philanthropy after their deaths.

And now, as I roam my gaze over the stud in front of me, he's part of that good work.

I shove all my desire for him under the carpet. This is about friendship and goals.

For both of us.

The date is simply a detail.

"You don't have to pay my share. I'll do it."

3

TEAGAN

He stares like I've announced I want to fly to Mars for vacation, camp out and eat Skittles on the red planet, then hop an interplanetary jet home.

"Don't be silly, King."

I cross my arms, holding my ground. "It's not silly. I want to. Also, hello? I need to. The King Family Foundation and all." My voice goes steely, as it sometimes does when I say that name, when I remember all that legacy encompasses.

"I know," he says, his voice soft and gentle. "But I would never ask you for a donation. That's just wrong."

"It's not wrong. It's literally what I do." I give a little foot stomp for emphasis.

He sets a hand on my arm, a tender sort of touch that surprises me. He's been touchier than usual tonight. Maybe I have too. "You'd be doing me a favor by bidding on me. I want to win for pride and for the cause," he says. "But no way am I asking you to pay for the date. That's not fair."

"North, here's the deal. Assuming I get board approval for the donation, I'm splitting the price tag with you. That's just how it's going to be. I want to pay for it. I want you to hit that goal, and I want our date to be covered on social media because that'll raise the profile of the foundation, as well as awareness of the work we're doing for companion dogs. So, that's my offer." I tap my toe, a move that's not terribly foreboding in pink Chuck Taylors, but so it goes. "What say you?"

He lets out a long stream of air, rubs a hand across his chin, then says, "You are ferocious in every single battle, King."

"Yes, and there is no zombie-laughter mulligan here."

"All right. Let's do this."

"Let's do it," I echo, then I nod to the stage, where Bryn and Logan are crooning *"Hooked on a Feeling."* So perfect for the two of them. It's their theme song, those lovebirds. "I think this calls for a song. And you get to pick which one," I say, tapping his shoulder.

"I won, so I picked the favor," he points out.

"I'm feeling generous. Pick the song too, North."

"If you insist."

His eyes sparkle with a glint that says he has something up his sleeve. We head to the stage, and when Bryn and Logan finish, Ransom scrolls through the song options on the screen, winks at me as he selects one, then hands me the mic.

When I see the screen, I crack up. Quickly, though, I

school my expression, draw a settling breath, and launch into "The Boy Is Mine," giving it my all.

He joins in, and we ham it up, strutting across the stage. I'm having a blast, like I usually do with Ransom.

Here and now, sure. But also because we're plotting something fun.

Something big.

Something good.

And then we'll go on a date.

And that'll be fun too.

But when I look at the crowd, my joy in the moment fizzles out, leaving me flat. It seems like everyone here is coupled up, arms draped around each other, heads resting on shoulders, kisses brushing cheeks. My heart aches at the sight.

I once wanted that.

I once had that.

But that kind of love cuts deep.

I wish it didn't. But, oh hell, does it ever.

Once, I'd felt those overwhelming, chest-flooding emotions, and the one I'd loved abandoned me when I needed him the most.

The chorus of the song comes in, and my throat catches. I swallow down the sadness and loss, shoving away this flood of emotion.

Then I glance at Ransom and go back to laughing, having a good time.

Yes, I'm the good-time girl.

He's the good-time guy.

That is who we are.

That is who we will always be.

* * *

At the end of the evening, as everyone shuffles off—hand in hand, arm in arm, lips ready to lock—I head outside with Ransom, telling him I'm going to wait for my Lyft.

"I'll wait with you," he says, with a softness in his eyes that I see every now and then.

"You don't have to."

"I want to, Teagan," he insists. "I want to make sure you get home safely."

"You have to protect your top bidder before the auction," I tease.

He tilts his head, rolling his eyes. "Yeah, that's it. No other reason."

I nudge him, keeping up the joke because humor is safer than being serious with him. "Don't worry. Just set me up with a bodyguard and around-the-clock protection, and I'll be fine."

"Good to know. Because my other alternative was to do that whole Han Solo encase-you-in-carbonite routine."

I wave a hand dismissively. "That's so 1981."

The Lyft arrives, and I slide inside, click the seat belt, and glance out the window. Ransom's eyes lock with mine, and for a fleeting second—okay, for maybe ten fleeting seconds—after he says my name and wishes me good night, I can kind of see why our friends are always trying to hook us up.

He's gorgeous, single, funny, and talented, and he doesn't want to be serious.

I don't do serious either.

Maybe they all figure we're perfect clowns together. That we'd be perfectly unserious together.

Maybe they're right, because he's a lot like me.

But what would happen if two people who didn't want to be serious got together? They'd crash into each other for a hot, fiery moment in time. Then they'd repel each other.

We'd become that annoying couple who dated once and then hated each other.

We'd become the bruise in our group of friends, the brown hole in the apple that you try to avoid.

I won't do that to my friends. I love them too much. They have been my family since my family has been gone.

That's why I email Nancy in the cab on the way home, extending my donation request to include the companion dog organization, and I go home alone—as I've done for years.

The next morning, Nancy emails me back to tell me the board for my parents' foundation approved a bid for the companion dog charity.

Then I read the amount she's nominated.

My jaw drops.

There's no way anyone else will be taking Ransom home.

I get out of bed and head to the kitchen, stopping at

a framed photo of my family on the way, a shot of the four of us from more than twenty years ago.

Back when my family was a foursome.

The least I can do is carry on their wishes, to take all this money they earned and give most of it away.

And maybe, just maybe, along the way, I'll have a Sunday Funday–type date with the most interesting man I know. But that'll be all. Because there's nothing more brewing between us.

There *shouldn't* be anything else brewing but the coffee I'm starting in the kitchen.

With the coffee maker gurgling, I grab my phone and send a morning hello to Bryn, ready to give her a piece of my mind, even if it's a playful one.

Teagan: You are such a troublemaker.

Bryn: *Moi?*

Teagan: Don't act so innocent.

Bryn: Ha. As if I'm innocent of anything.

Teagan: Exactly.

Bryn: But what is this trouble you speak of, my friend?

Teagan: I know that you and Fitz and Logan and Summer and Oliver engineered this whole auction date thing with Ransom.

Bryn: Hmm. That's quite an allegation. Any evidence to prove your accusation?

I roll my eyes at her reply, laughing as I take down a coffee mug. Then I write back.

Teagan: It's adorable that you think I didn't immediately know you were the puppeteer in all of this. *Hey, how about Teagan bids on Ransom? Gee, won't that be perfect?* So you. So very you.

Bryn: But did you see me working the strings?

Teagan: I did. Right along with Fitz. You two, I swear.

Bryn: Fine. What can I say? We can both see what's RIGHT IN FRONT OF US!!

Teagan: What's in front of you is a dreamscape. You live in some friendship fantasia.

Bryn: Stop ruining my cupid dreams.

Teagan: My dream is for all of us to have brunch on Sunday, no weirdness on the menu.

Bryn: Fine. Fine. We'll do brunch.

Teagan: And to keep doing brunch. I like brunch. I like our crew. I like the status quo.

Bryn: Message received—don't rock the boat. Sourpuss.

Teagan: Aww, I love you too.

Bryn: Love you more.

I pour some coffee, take a sip, and check my Tinder profile. Scroll, scroll, scroll.

Nobody catches my interest.

Nobody looks like someone I'd want to commit to grabbing a latte with, let alone spend an evening with.

Leaving the phone on the counter, I take my mug and move to the living room window, gazing out at the tree-lined block on the Upper East Side.

My home. My parents' home before it was mine.

And outside of this home are all my friends that make this city, this life, these times work for me.

Bryn, Ransom, Logan, Fitz, Dean, Summer, Oliver. The whole crew.

An auction is an auction is an auction.

That is all.

And everything will be fine.

4

RANSOM

My friends are competitive assholes.

That's a fact I accept. Embrace, really, since I'm one of them.

We compete over everything.

And fine, maybe I need to extend my definition of "friends" past my paintball-karaoke-darts-playing group. Maybe my competitors on the Yankees *are* friends.

But I need to keep them mentally in the frenemy zone so I can win the big prize—their money.

Plus bragging rights, of course.

That Saturday, after I get dressed and button up my tuxedo shirt, I text the dickheads on the Yankees, starting with Martinez, the closer.

Ransom: Marty Boy, did you convince your sister to bid on you yet?

Martinez: No, I convinced your sister. Last night.

I stare, narrow-eyed, at the text. Yeah, I walked into that. But there is no way he could ever score with Tempest. I toss a glance behind me at my younger sister —electric-blue glasses, hair twisted into a bun and held with a pencil as she chews the corner of her lip and taps away on her laptop in my living room. She's been hanging here for the last couple of hours, since it's a Saturday and she works both *Hamilton* shows.

"Temp, you don't think Martinez is hot, do you?"

She crinkles her nose and scrunches her brow, her face doing a hula dance of confusion. "Who's that? One of those one-name actors? Is he on *Scrubs*?"

"*Scrubs* has been off the air for years. Good job, Ms. Anti Pop Culture."

"I know Broadway."

"That does not count as pop culture."

"Millions of *Hamilton* fans would beg to differ."

"Fine," I concede. "*Hamilton* is pop culture."

"Is he one of your teammates? Because Martinez isn't ringing a bell."

I snort. "Marty Boy wishes he were talented enough to play hockey."

"Now I'm curious about this guy. Marty Boy, you say?"

"That's only what I call him because it drives him bananas."

"What's his first name?"

"Adrian. Adrian Martinez."

Something shifts in her expression, like her brain unlocked with a click. "Wait. The guy you've been calling Marty Boy is really Adrian Martinez? As in Adrian Martinez of the Yankees?"

"So you do know him?"

"He's definitely not on *Scrubs*. But let me just make sure he's who I'm thinking of."

She cracks her knuckles above the keys before she taps away, mouthing, *Who is Adrian Martinez?*

I groan. Why did I say his name? Now she'll look him up, and I know what she'll see—the guy who's numero uno on a bunch of lists of hottest single athletes in New York.

Yes, I follow that sort of shit. The Dating Pool, Buzz-Feed, City Post. Because then I can give my asshole friends a hard time.

Grabbing my bow tie, I return to the text thread, since the smack talk force is strong in me.

Ransom: I see you're still taking hallucinogenic drugs. Keep it up, Martinez. I cannot wait to beat your sorry ass tonight when I take home the grand prize as the top fundraising athlete.

Martinez: Understandable. You couldn't nab top honors on the City Post list, so you gotta try for them where you can.

He sends a photo of his face, so naturally I have to respond like this.

Ransom: Awesome. Gonna go put this on a mug now, along with a cartoon bubble caption that says "Ransom North is my idol."

Martinez: You do that. Then let me know how it feels to constantly come in third place to Carnale and me. Want me to send some tissues for your tears? Or should I make it some towels because you're probably drowning in a pool?

Ransom: Be sure to bring blankets to sop up your waterworks tonight, dickhead, when I win all your money.

Martinez: A few too many hits on the ice has made your head too big, North. Or is it that your dick is small, since you play a sport less popular?

Ransom: My dick is double digits. And my contract has plenty of zeros. Case in point: I do believe that's my face I walked past earlier today in Times Square, advertising watches. Take that.

Martinez: Was it beneath my underwear ad?

I groan, dragging a hand through my hair. I forgot about his billboard too. His fucking billboard, which is right above mine. Dammit.

My sister snaps her fingers. "Why didn't you tell me *your* Martinez was Adrian Alejandro Martinez from the Gigante underwear ad in Times Square?"

I hang my head. "I should never have mentioned his name," I mutter.

"Oh, you should have. Believe me, you should have. God bless you, big brother. I didn't connect the dots. But now I'd like to play connect the dots on him. And Battleship. And Chutes and Ladders. I mean, look at those abs," she says, spinning her laptop around and shoving it at me. It's open to a full-screen image of the Yankees closer dressed only in a pair of royal-blue briefs and a smirk. "I have no interest in athletes, but I think I might make this my new wallpaper."

I stare at the ceiling. "What have I done?"

"You've introduced me to my new eye candy, so thank you very much." She eyes my phone. "Is he the one you're trash-talking to?"

"No," I scoff.

Setting her computer down, she rises and makes grabby hands. "Liar."

I raise my phone above my head. She's not short, but I'm six foot three, so lifting the device out of her reach is no sweat. "How do you know I was trash-talking?"

She rolls her eyes as she tries to snag the phone, a futile but amusing attempt. "It's only your favorite hobby of all time," she says, finally giving up and lowering her arms. Returning to the couch, she closes her computer and slides it into her black messenger bag. She's a financial whiz and a brilliant writer, so she pens columns for various money magazines, as well as authoring personal finance books, a gig that frees her up to do what she truly loves—interpreting Broadway shows and other performances for the deaf and hard of hearing.

I tuck my phone into my pocket and finish with my bow tie, conceding she's right. "Look. I only trash-talk Carnale and Martinez because they deserve it. That's why I have to take them down tonight."

"Why do they deserve trash talk and a takedown?" she asks with a furrowed brow.

"Duh. Because they're Yankees," I say. Isn't it obvious?

"And that's the only reason?" She slings her bag across her chest as I grab my keys, tossing them high in the air and catching them easily.

"What other reason do I need?"

She arches a brow. "Is it because of the lists they're on?"

"What lists?" I ask, like I have no clue what she means.

She shakes her head as she rolls her eyes. "You're so see-through. You're like a cellophane brother," she says as we exit my corner apartment.

"And what do you see when you look through the Saran Wrap of me, Temp?"

She frames her eyes with her hands. "You're jealous because those two guys are jockeying for one and two on the hot lists and you're a consistent three."

I dismiss that crazy notion. "As if I care about those lists."

"You always care, and I know why." Her tone is a little softer, a little gentler.

"Because *they* care," I blurt. But that's not all of it, and she does know the rest.

"*Ransom.*"

"Whatever. It's just a game."

As we wait for the elevator, she sets a hand on my arm. "It's because of Edie."

I cringe. "No."

"*Ransom.*"

I sigh heavily. "Whatever. I don't care about her."

"You didn't care about those lists until she left."

"Because I wasn't on them when I was with her. Because I was *involved*," I bite out.

"I know," she says softly. "But really, what difference does it make if you're one, two, or three? Any woman with her head on straight would be thrilled to have you, regardless of the number. Edie didn't see what was in front of her, and she lost out."

"Well, I don't want to be *had*," I say as the elevator arrives, the doors sliding open. "This guy is happy to be single."

"Maybe someday you'll want a relationship again."

"Maybe never. And until then, it's way more fun to bust my buddies' chops on these single-in-the-city lists, because being single means I can do whatever I want."

It also means no one can ever again hurt me like Edie did the night I proposed to her two years ago.

The night she told me she'd fallen in love with another man.

For four years, I was devoted to her.

Four years flushed down the drain in a single night, along with a ring I never gave her.

"You really don't ever want to get involved again?" Tempest asks.

As the doors shut and I press the button for the lobby, I shoot her a warning look. She knows the answer. She's asked me the question often enough.

"I don't," I say quietly. "It's not worth it. I don't want to go through that ever again."

Tempest squeezes my shoulder. "I get that it doesn't feel worth it. She really did a number on you."

I shrug it off. "Nah. I'm all good. And you know what else is good and fun?" I wiggle my brows. "Trash talk."

Rolling her eyes, she sighs in loud exasperation. "*Boys.* Can you please explain why trash talk is so singularly motivating to your gender?"

I shrug. "We have penises."

We reach the lobby and step out of the elevator as she mutters, "Gross."

"Aww, do penises gross you out, Temp?"

She gives me a droll look. "Yours does."

I gesture to the lobby as if to indicate the entire building. "Why is it you come here between shows again?"

"Your place is closer to the theater district. Also, now that I've seen Adrian's picture, I'm worried you're not hot enough to win tonight. Do you want me to grab a mask for you at the party supply store? Maybe a clown or an ex-president?"

I'm relieved she's moved on from the subject of Edie and returned to our brother-sister banter.

I arch a brow. "You do know where I learned to smack-talk?"

"From the best of them." With a twinkle in her eye, she points her thumb at herself. "Me."

"Exactly. Mouth of vitriol. And speaking of your acid tongue, you can take all those remarks back about Martinez. You're not allowed to think he's hot," I hiss as we pass the doorman. I take a second to nod hello though. "Hey, Oscar. How's it going? How did Melissa do in her lacrosse tournament?"

"Came in first place, sir. Thanks for asking."

"Awesome news." I smile and wave as we head onto Park Avenue.

When we hit the street, Tempest jumps back into it. "I take it back. Martinez isn't hot."

I grin, nice and satisfied. "Exactly."

She smirks at me, satisfied as a cat, then she whispers, "He's *smoking* hot."

I groan. "You have no taste."

"I have amazing taste. Maybe I should go to the auction tonight?"

"You wouldn't dare."

"I wouldn't dare bid on him?" She cocks a brow.

"You wouldn't dare miss *Hamilton*."

"Oh, I *might* miss *Hamilton* to bid on a guy that smoking hot, and there's nothing you could do to stop me."

She's right. There is nada I could do to stop her. Because that's not how I roll. She's free to do what she wants, date who she wants, and see who she wants.

Obviously.

Still, the ribbing I would endure in that scenario would be immeasurable.

"Just promise me if you go out with him that—"

"I say nice things about you?"

I roll my eyes. "Sisters. Pretend I never said a word."

"That's generally my MO." She blows me a kiss. "Love you."

"Love you too, Temp."

"Also, I would never skip a show to bid on a guy, so you don't have to worry," she adds.

I breathe a genuine sigh of relief. "Good to know."

As I grab my phone to call a Lyft, she raises her hands and signs rapidly in ASL, "But say hi to Adrian tonight from me."

I growl, sneering at her as I stuff my phone into my pocket with one hand and sign with the other. "Never."

"I'll meet him on my own, then." Words fly from her hands. "I'd totally do him."

I sign again. "You are the pig now."

She laughs, tossing her head back, speaking this time. "Good luck, Ransom. I need to get to the theater."

"Spoiler. Hamilton dies. Burr kills him."

She lifts her hands and signs once more. "Oh my God, I had no idea, dickhead."

I grab her and wrap her in a hug. "See you tomorrow. Luna's house? I won't tell her you've been swearing and casting aspersions in ASL."

Tempest laughs. "She's the one who taught us those words."

We say goodbye as my Lyft arrives, and I head to Teagan's place in the East Eighties, bounding up the steps to her brownstone, one of those gorgeous homes with red brick and polished white shutters. It's like a set from a movie, the house where the well-heeled New Yorker lives.

Which is fitting, since I know she comes from money. Old money.

I call to let her know I'm here. I half want to head upstairs to gawk at whatever her pad looks like, but once the door opens, all thoughts free-fall from my brain and land on the sidewalk.

5

RANSOM

Holy purple dress.

Holy black heels.

Holy red hair swept up in a French twist thingy.

I grab the railing, since I nearly fall backward.

Which is not something I normally do, thanks to my catlike reflexes. It's literally my job to react in a nanosecond.

Trouble is, I'm stunned speechless by the beauty in front of me.

The dress clings deliciously to her body. Some kind of soft, flowy material shows off her arms, hugs her hips, and reveals her legs.

"You look incredible." My voice sounds huskier than it should.

Smokier.

I swallow roughly, trying to get past the dry patch in my throat.

But I don't know if I want to. All I want is to drink her up, gawk at her.

Memorize how she looks in purple.

"You clean up okay too," she says, bright and chipper, the tone a reminder that we are friends.

Right.

Yup.

I should not be staring at her like I want to discover what her lipstick tastes like.

This is not a date. It won't even be a real date if she wins me. We're going as friends, and friends only.

But fuck me.

Friends are not supposed to look so good in sexy, slinky dresses.

What was I thinking, asking her to bid on me? How the hell am I going to make it through tonight without telling her I want to toss her over my shoulder, take her home, kiss the hollow of her throat, then work my way down her lush body? That I want to savor the taste of her skin and adore the feel of her curves?

I cycle back, realizing that words have come out of that sexy mouth. Words that need a response. What were they?

Ah, yes. I clean up okay.

How would someone not be dumbstruck by her reply?

"Thanks," I say.

Wow. Well done, brain. That was just brilliant.

"Want to see something cool?" she asks from where we still stand outside her door. I can't move. My feet are rooted to the top step.

"Sure," I say, gritting my teeth, telling myself to stop lusting after my friend.

Friends are off-limits.

That's my goddamn mantra.

"I practiced my lines for tonight. Check this out." She thrusts her right arm high in the air and declares, "One million dollars!"

That does the trick. Her humor. Her lightness. It settles the tension in me so that it falls away and I can talk again, move again.

I gesture to the steps, and we walk down to the sidewalk. "I love charity, but I don't have that kind of jack."

She frowns. "Are you sure?"

"I'm positive."

"Hmm. Okay, how about this?" She clears her throat, lifts a finger daintily, and affixes a most serious expression on her face. "I bid two dollars on Ransom North."

As we walk toward Madison, I laugh. "Try somewhere in between, King."

She nudges my arm with her elbow. "Don't you worry. I'm going to nab you tonight. I'm determined." She rubs her palms together, and we review the bidding plan. That helps center me too, underlines the definition of who we are.

When we finish, she asks, "So why this charity?"

Funny that I've known her for months but the question has never come up before. This is a good enough time to talk about it, since it isn't a deep, dark secret. "My older sister, Luna . . ."

"The pretty blonde? The one who's married?"

"How do you know she's blonde?"

Teagan rolls her eyes. "Hello? Social media strategist here. I've seen pictures of your family at your games.

During the playoffs, you posted a pic on Instagram of your parents and your two sisters cheering you on. There was a dog in the shot too. Well, a dog face."

I laugh, a little embarrassed. "Oh, yeah. Well, there is that."

"Also, I'm not a stalker. But I happen to have a thing for dog photos."

I nod exaggeratedly. "'I'm not a stalker' is what everyone who's a stalker says."

She pats her chest. "Dog-lover, Ransom. I'm a dog lover. Anyway, continue."

"Luna lost most of her hearing when she was younger—around two or three—so my whole family knows sign language. She's also the reason I want to raise the most money. Because companion dogs are awesome, and my sister's Lab helps her every day. That was Angela at the game—the Lab."

"Her dog's name is Angela?"

"Yes."

Teagan brings a hand to her heart. "I love her already."

I furrow my brow. "The dog or my sister?"

"Both. I love human names for dogs." Teagan beams, a big, warm smile. "Also, I think that's amazing."

"That she has a service dog?"

She shakes her head. "No. That you want to do this for her, raise more for a charity that matters to her and her life. To your family. That's cool. Also, hello, hidden talent." She flashes me a smile. "You know another language."

"True. That is another of my hidden talents," I say.

"Thank you for sharing that with me." Her tone gentles as she says it, her smile soft and inviting. "I assume it's not a secret, but I also know sometimes it's hard to share details about our families. I appreciate it."

"Sometimes it's hard, but sometimes it's easy," I say, although it's rarely difficult to talk to Teagan. "It's easy talking to you, and that's not the case with everyone."

When people find out I know sign language or that my sister can't hear, they sometimes want to delve too deep, ask all sorts of questions that aren't their business. *How do you feel about that? How was that growing up? What was it like when you were all kids?*

What was it like? It was like my life. Her life. *Our* life. It was all normal to me, plain and simple.

It's who we are, my family. We laugh and joke and tease and love. My sisters and me, my parents and us.

I like that Teagan isn't whispering intrusive questions at me, or giving me that *I'm so sorry* look.

Instead, she asks something simple about my everyday life. "You must use ASL every time you're with your sister, then. Do you use it elsewhere?"

That's much easier to answer. "I do volunteer work with some little kids who have hearing loss. I help with reading, but I can sign if they need me to."

She brings her hand to her heart. "You're making me melt. That's amazing. Big, strong hockey player signing to kids. Ransom, that's incredible."

I wave a hand, even as my chest warms. "It's nothing."

She shakes her head. "It's not nothing. That's inspiring. And it's something unexpected."

"From an athlete?"

"Well, yeah," she says matter-of-factly. "I'm sure it means a lot to the kids and their parents."

"That's what they tell me, but honestly, that's not why I do it. And I don't put it on social media, because I don't want the focus to be on me. I just want to help the kids. I know from Luna how beneficial it is to talk to others."

She beams. "I love it. I would love to know some words."

"Maybe I'll teach you sometime."

"I look forward to that."

My heart glows a little from this conversation, from her interest and her admiration, but I don't want to linger in this self-congratulatory zone.

We turn down Madison, through Saturday evening crowds, walking past couples dressed up for dates, weaving through throngs of friends decked out for a night on the town, and when I have the chance, I shift the focus back to her.

"Let's turn the tables," I say as my opening move.

She nods crisply. "Table turning, I am ready. What have you got?"

"Your parents' foundation. I know the basics from the website, but I'd like to know more."

She snaps her gaze toward me as we slow at a light. "You visited the foundation's page?"

"This surprises you? That I know how to use the internet?"

She shakes her head, then replies, her voice soft, "Not that part, Ransom."

My heart squeezes, and I fear I've said the wrong thing, made light of something at the wrong time. "Sorry, Teagan. I didn't mean to joke."

She doesn't answer right away, just knits her brow. Then she draws a deep breath. "I was just surprised you looked it up. I don't know why though. I think it caught me off guard."

"I was honestly just curious about you," I say, gentling my tone to match her shift in mood. "Trying to understand what makes you tick."

Her lips relax into a soft smile, and then she shakes her head. "Hey, don't apologize. I'm actually sort of touched."

And now I'm surprised too. Seems like we're both catching each other off guard tonight. "Why are you touched?"

She shrugs lightly. "Just that you made the effort. That means a lot to me, that you took an interest." She clears her throat, her lips going straight, her eyes more serious. "My mother and little sister died in a car crash when I was twenty. My sister, Millie, was eight."

Her voice is calm, but almost too perfectly modulated, as if she's practiced keeping it that way. How else could she get out such horrors? My heart craters for her, at the thought of what she's gone through.

"And then my father passed away three years ago. Heart disease." She swallows roughly and then finishes, "Which seemed like exactly what would kill him. A broken heart."

She wobbles on those last words, and my throat seizes as a tide of emotion wells up, a swell of sympathy.

I set a hand on her back, rubbing gently as we walk. "Shit, Teagan. I'm so sorry. I knew your parents were gone. But I didn't realize you had a little sister and that she died too. That is horrible."

She nods quickly, screwing up the corner of her lips. "It was pretty terrible."

We stop where the light is red at the crosswalk, and I don't think, I just do. I wrap her in a hug. "That's a lot to go through. I'm so sorry for your loss."

She laughs, trying to make light of it, I suspect. "Oh, stop. No pity hugs."

I hug her tighter, going for humor. "My hugs are not pitiful."

"Fine, your pitiful hugs are decent," she grumbles.

"Yes, I am a very decent hugger," I say, laughing.

I don't let her go, and she doesn't seem to want me to. Her arms slide tightly around my waist, and we stand that way, there in the middle of the city. This embrace is completely out of character for both of us, but perhaps it's entirely necessary.

"Thank you, Ransom. For . . . everything."

I'm not sure what I did, or what she's thanking me for. But I don't care, since she's warm and soft in my arms, and she feels so good. Maybe it's wrong to enjoy a hug so much after an emotional moment. But if this is wrong, I don't want to be right.

Except, as I breathe in her soft strawberry scent, I remind myself of my lines.

My limits.

The longer the embrace lasts, the more I want to

smell her hair, slide my nose along the soft skin of her neck, inhale her.

But those lines are there for a reason.

So that I don't make the same mistakes I made with Edie.

Falling for a friend nearly cost me my sanity.

When Edie left me, I spiraled like I never had before.

I can't go there again.

I won't go there again.

That's a chance I simply won't take.

I break the hug, then cuff Teagan playfully on the arm. "All right, King. Let's get the bidding going."

She smiles. "Two million dollars."

All I can do is shake my head and laugh.

We continue on to Sixtieth Street, turn the corner, and head into the swank Luxe Hotel. Teagan excuses herself for the restroom, and as I wait in the hallway, a booming voice echoes down the corridor.

"Does anyone know what time it is?"

I turn around to see the smug face of Adrian Martinez as he walks my way, tossing out the tagline from my Times Square ad.

But I can do him one better. His billboard might be big, and his flesh might be on display front and center, but the Gigante tagline is ripe for riffing on.

"Hey," I call, matching his taunting tone. "If it isn't *the only thing a man wants against his body.*"

Adrian rolls his eyes. "Dude."

"Dude," I repeat.

"I didn't write the motherfucking tagline," he says.

"If you did, it would be: *Check me out in Underoos.*"

For some reason, that cracks the man up. He laughs, big and deep, and offers me a fist for knocking. "You're an asshole, North, and I am going to take you down, but you are one funny as fuck hideous beast."

"Right back atcha."

"Who's the hideous beast?" Teagan asks as she rejoins us.

When Adrian's eyes swing to her, his baby blues flicker to the tune of *Whoa, who the hell is this babe?*

Out of nowhere, a green-eyed dragon roars inside me, breathing fire and thrashing.

"Hello there. I'm Adrian Martinez," he says, going all smooth, like he's about to hit on her. He extends a hand. "Pleasure to meet you."

She shakes it, and I burn inside.

I do not want anyone else touching Teagan King, and that's a brand-new feeling.

A fucking inconvenient one too.

6

TEAGAN

He's towering.

I'm guessing he's six foot twenty.

No wonder Adrian terrifies opposing batters. He has eyes like ice. They're crystal blue, and they're stunning.

I have no doubt he's going to go for a million pretty pennies. Yet he has nothing on Ransom.

The man next to me is simply . . . delicious.

Even more so after our chat on the way over.

And I know how badly Ransom wants to beat these guys. Hell, I want him to. If we do, we can raise even more money for his chosen charity.

The look in Ransom's eyes—fiery—tells me he wants me to play along with the whole *we pretend to hate each other* pretense.

But I decide to have a little fun with these guys.

I shake Adrian's hand, answering his question. "I'm Teagan King, and I happen to be a big fan of hideous beasts." Then I take Ransom's arm. "And he's the most hideous one of all," I say, in a way that makes it clear he's the complete opposite of grotesque.

"Oh, I love it when you call me names, dollface," Ransom says with a twinkle in his eyes.

I give an over-the-top pout, tapping my finger against his nose. "You adore everything I do, my beast."

He smiles all lovey-dovey. "I so do."

Adrian furrows his brow, pointing from Ransom to me and back. "Hey, Puck Boy, I didn't know you had a girlfriend till I saw you walk in with this *belleza*. How the hell is that possible?"

I flick my gaze to Ransom, and he shoots one back at me. A look that says, *Go along with it.*

Because that's what these guys do. They one-up each other. That's their hobby.

I squeeze Ransom a little tighter. "What can I say? He's irresistible, and that's why I came here tonight. Can't let any other woman get her claws in this guy, can I now?"

"I don't think anyone would want to," Adrian says, but then he flashes me a grin. "Now tell me, Teagan. Are you honestly a fan of the world's dullest sport?"

"Yes, *are* you a fan of long, dull games played on baseball diamonds, Teagan?" Ransom asks pointedly. "Inquiring minds want to know."

I smile at Martinez, giving a *my bad* laugh. "Oh, when you said 'dullest sport,' I thought you meant auto racing."

The Yankee chuckles and points at me. "She's a keeper, Ransom. Don't let this one get away."

Ransom shoots me a sweet smile, then shrugs. "I won't."

A waiter circles by.

"Want to grab some drinks?" Martinez asks.

"See? I knew you guys were friends," I say.

Martinez narrows his eyes.

Ransom hisses.

I roll my eyes. "You can't fool me. But I can go along with this whole frenemies thing if you want."

"Good answer, Teagan," Ransom says as he snags three flutes and thanks the server.

With champagne in hand, Martinez looks my way. "Moment of truth—what is your favorite sport, Teagan? But if you hate sports, please lie because that would devastate us." He smacks Ransom on the shoulder, and I love that too—the little signs that these guys really are buddies, even though they pretend they're not.

"I actually love baseball," I say truthfully.

Ransom jerks his gaze to me, blinking. "Blasphemy."

"What can I say? My dad was a huge fan, and we had season tickets for the Yankees," I tell them. "He took me to a ton of games back in the heyday of Jeter and Williams, Posada and Rivera."

Martinez brings his hand to his heart. "Those guys are my heroes. I watched them all late at night growing up across Europe, when I could get the games on satellite in Spain, Italy, sometimes in France. But wherever I was, one thing remained the same — Mariano Rivera is the greatest ever."

"He's the best. No one has ever been better."

"No question. I look up to him, to Posada—to all

those greats. It is an honor to play on the same team as the men I admired from across the ocean." Martinez turns to Ransom. "And I take back everything I've ever said about you because your girlfriend is an angel."

Ransom drapes an arm around me. "She's pretty awesome, isn't she?"

Martinez again looks from Ransom to me and back. Something seems to spark in the cool blue eyes of the closer. "May the best man win tonight." He downs some of his drink, then looks at his watch. "I should go freshen up before I have to strut onstage and crush your sorry ass. Carnale and I have our own side bet about the auction."

"Oh, yeah? What's it for?"

Martinez tips his chin at me. "When we saw you come in, Carnale laid a grand on the charity of your choice that your girlfriend won't kiss you backstage if you win. I said she would. Guess we'll find out soon enough."

He winks, claps Ransom on the shoulder, and strolls away.

In slow motion, Ransom turns to me, and when our eyes lock, neither one of us seems to know what to say.

I don't know if I can speak.

All I can do is wonder.

I wonder what that kiss with him would be like.

When his eyes darken, flaring with something that looks like heat, I wonder how much he wants to know too.

* * *

A few hours later, when Ransom heads backstage, I make a beeline for the women's room. Peeing, obvs. Then washing my hands. Double obvs. I touch up my gloss, check my hair, and take a breath.

I'm a little nervous, and I'm not a nervous person. So, I turn to *my person*.

Bryn.

I take out my phone and send a quick text. She's my de facto family, my best friend. We met a few years ago in a grief support group. We'd both lost our parents. We were both alone. We needed each other. Our friendship was born from the ashes of others' lives.

Teagan: Your crazy friend is ready to bid on your other crazy friend. Gah.

Bryn: Did you bring your piggy bank?

Teagan: Yes, and a hammer to smash it open. It'll be like performance art right in the middle of an auction.

Bryn: Never a dull moment with you, girl. But I have to ask—are you okay?

Teagan: Of course. Why?

Bryn: The *gah*. You always say "gah" when you're . . .

My phone trills in my hand, and I answer immediately. "Hey, girlie girl," I say, keeping it light.

"That's yet another giveaway." Bryn really does know me too well.

"Ugh. I hate you and your mind-reader ways," I say with a huff, leaning against the wall.

"What's wrong? Why are you nervous? Do you feel like we pushed you guys together?"

I roll my eyes. "You're always pushing us together."

"Yes, because you two are the perfect couple," she says, like it's as factual as Newton's Law of Universal Gravitation.

"I don't belong with anyone, and you know that," I say, sharp but clear. Because I'm not a one-person-or-bust kind of girl.

She sighs. "I know. I know. But maybe someday."

"Doubtful."

"So, why are you out of sorts?"

I roll my shoulders, trying to let go of the worries skating through me. "Eh, it's just momentary nerves. Ransom is so competitive, and he wants to win this, and I want to win this. For the foundation, for his fundraising. That's all."

She's quiet at first, then she asks, "Are you sure it's not for any other reason?"

A reason like I really dig the guy? Yes, I'm sure that's the reason. I'm positive. I'm damn positive, especially after that kiss comment, because I want to lay one on him and kiss him all night long. And maybe, just maybe, he wants that too. But then what would happen tomorrow?

"Just momentary nerves. Silly little things. Bye-bye, nerves."

"Let me know how it goes."

"I promise. Love you."

"Love you."

I end the call. Good thing she reached out. Talking to her reminds me what matters most.

My friends. *Our* friends. The whole family we've made in this city. These fluttery feelings aren't worth jeopardizing that.

So, I leave them all behind and head into the auction.

* * *

It's time.

I'm in the ballroom with hundreds of other dolled-up women and some spiffy men too. The Yankees shortstop is one of a few openly gay major league baseball players, and he's notoriously single too, so I'm not surprised the men are lining up to bid on him.

I survey the crowd, assessing the competition, trying to glean an idea of who might be vying for Ransom tonight.

Maybe that brunette in the red dress? She's studying a program for the night, and from where I sit, it looks like the page is open to the hockey players—three from Ransom's team.

Or the blonde with her hair in a sexy-messy bun? It looks like she has hockey sticks as nail art, which shows some serious commitment.

Nerves skitter across my skin, but I try to rid them with a healthy dose of determination.

I draw a breath, steeling myself.

It could be anyone. Could be a guy too. But whoever is gunning for the forward, I'm going to run the table.

That's the plan.

I'm going to get my man.

I'll make the biggest bid for Ransom. I have no control over what anyone else goes for, but I can do my damnedest to win him for a kiss.

I mean, for a cause.

Win him for the cause.

I repeat that over and over in my head.

Don't want to forget why I'm here.

The hostess—a polished and poised sports reporter from Las Vegas—strides across the stage.

"What a thrill to see so many of you here ready to bid on New York's finest men! I'm Lily Nichols, and I couldn't be more honored to host this year's charity auction," she says in a voice I know from her on-air reports. "We have quite a lineup tonight, so let's get started with some of the New York Giants."

She introduces the running back from the team, who strides onstage, flashing a smoldering smile and filling out a suit quite nicely. The audience hoots and hollers for the man as Lily rattles off Leon's attributes. "Leon loves to sing in the shower, spend time with his grandparents, and try new cuisines. Let the bidding begin."

After some heated back-and-forth bidding, Leon

goes for four digits, and some of the other football stars net a bigger payday before Lily segues to the NBA.

After she works her way through a handful of hoops players, she's on to the Yankees, talking up Jose Carnale.

I tap my toe, wishing the hockey guys were next.

"Jose Carnale loves to dance, run you a bubble bath, and hear about your day." Lily shoots the catcher an approving look. The strapping Bronx Bomber wiggles a brow. "My God, could this man be any more perfect?"

A determined Lucy Liu look-alike calls out, "He's mine!"

Time proves she is, indeed, determined. She wins him for a high four figures.

Next up is the team's shortstop, and the bidding war is fierce, with a smoldering man in a suit winning him, and all I can think is they'd make a smoking-hot couple. I hope their date turns into the real thing because I wouldn't mind checking out some cute couple pics from those two.

Purely as a social media strategist, of course.

"And now, we have The Tree, also known as Adrian Martinez, the star closer for the New York Yankees. An avid feline fan, every night he's in town, he goes home to his two cats, Puss and Boots."

The woman in front of me squeaks. The woman next to her gasps.

Understandable. Those are adorable names for kitties.

"He loves to cook for you, play Scrabble, and indulge in candlelit dinners."

Part of me wants to call bullshit. I mean, who really

likes all that? But the marketer in me is impressed. Adrian—or his press person—has made himself seem like quite a prize.

And maybe he is.

"Who would like to start the bidding?" Lily asks the audience.

A leggy lady in front of me thrusts her hand in the air. "I have a bidder on the phone," she says. When she drops the number, my jaw comes unhinged.

Damn.

That's a lot of greenbacks.

Before Lily can even ask if anyone else wants to meet it, one of the cat-lovers in front of me tosses her hat in the ring with a higher bid.

They go back and forth for a few minutes until the gasper drops out, and the anonymous phone bidder wins.

Martinez was the last Yankee. It's our turn now.

My stomach churns. Or maybe it flips. Hell, it might do both. I'm nervous and excited. Ready and worried.

Lily smiles, sweeps her arm out wide, and flashes a grin at the man in the tux who picked me up at my home earlier tonight.

"And we have Ransom North, star forward for this city's NHL franchise," she says as Ransom strides across the stage, a gorgeous smile gracing his hand-some face.

That smile.

My God. It's so magnetic. So inviting. So warm. All at the same time. His dimples are killing me, making me feel all gooey inside.

He scans the crowd and finds me. A twinkle seems to play across his hazel eyes.

My heart stutters.

Flippity-flop.

My cheeks flush.

Burn, baby, burn.

And my pulse? It freaking races.

Cheetah fast.

"I want to have your children, Ransom!"

I blink, jerking my gaze toward the source of the high-pitched warrior whoop—a freckled woman in a white dress coos at Ransom from the back row.

"How about we start by trying to win a dinner?" Lily asks diplomatically.

"Dinner then making babies." The lady does a pump of her hips—impressive, given that she's sitting down.

Okay, then.

Lily shakes her head. "Let's remember to stay classy, everyone." She returns to her list. "Ransom North loves to play Ping-Pong with his friends, read fast-paced thrillers, volunteer with children who have hearing loss, and help with companion dogs. He also has quite a sweet tooth and says he can easily be bribed to do extra chores . . . with a chocolate milkshake."

I laugh at the bio, the things I knew—Ping-Pong and kids—and also the thing I didn't—his affinity for milkshakes.

"Who would like to start the bidding?"

I raise my hand and toss out my opening bid.

The woman in white raises me by a small amount.

We go back and forth, with others weighing in too.

As I up the bid once more, a tall figure weaves through the crowd. Is that . . .?

Oh, my stars.

It is.

Fitz.

And he's not alone.

He's flanked by Logan and Oliver. The three of them make their way toward the front row, with Fitz raising his hand.

"I'll make an offer on North," he booms, then outbids me by one thousand dollars.

Ransom's eyes widen, and he tilts his head, giving his buddy a *what's up* look.

My potential date's eyes swing to me, and he nods at me with narrowed eyes.

I'm not positive what that nod means, but knowing him, I'm going to assume it means *win at all costs*.

I raise my hand, and with all the bravado I have—and that's a lot—I up the bid.

Fitz laughs and does me better, going higher.

What the hell?

Do these guys not know me?

I'm not about to be outbid by Ransom's friends.

He's mine. Oh hell, is he ever mine.

Squaring my shoulders, I raise the stakes.

Fitz rolls his eyes, lifts a casual finger, and adds another thousand. Out of the corner of my eye, I spot Martinez leaning against the wall, chuckling.

"We've got quite a bidding war going. I guess you both want to get milkshakes with Ransom, and it looks like"—Lily stops, peers into the audience, and does a double take when she sees who's in on the action—"last year's winner is in the lead. James Fitzgerald."

Last year's winner.

And those words click in my head.

They flash brightly.

Because I'm pretty sure that's not allowed.

I'm willing to bet Lily's pause means she thinks so too.

I clear my throat and decide to go for it. Our friends are messing with me, but I know how to mess right back. "Excuse me, Lily, but are we sure that former entrants in the auction are allowed to bid on other entrants?"

"I'll bid on him," Oliver chimes in.

"Me too. He's worth a couple bucks," Logan puts in.

Lily flashes a professional grin. "He's worth plenty, but since Fitzgerald began the bidding, he's responsible for it."

She steps into the wings, and I cannot suppress a smile as she confers with the organizer.

Ransom grins at me from his spot onstage.

Seconds later, Lily's heels click across the hardwood, and she scans the crowd for the guys. "As much as we appreciate your bid, Mr. Fitzgerald, you are, in fact, disqualified." She turns to the crowd. "Do we have any other bids for Ransom North?"

She waits, checking out the room.

I cross my fingers.

I hope he's mine for so many reasons—first and foremost because he's about to go for more moolah than the other guys.

And secondly because . . . I want to make him happy.

And this will make him happy.

"Going, going, gone. To the redhead in the second row."

I double-pump my fists.

Ransom blows me a kiss.

Then Fitz smiles at me and winks at Martinez.

Martinez swings his gaze from Ransom to me, and his words from earlier echo in my mind, loud and crystal clear.

But did they ever really fade away?

Carnale laid a grand on the charity of your choice that your girlfriend won't kiss you backstage if you win. I said she would. Guess we'll find out soon enough.

That's the question indeed. Will I?

* * *

When the auction ends, the guys are gone, Fitz, Logan, and Oliver having bid and run.

The winners, meanwhile, go to greet the players backstage. Ransom strides over to me, heat in his eyes. My stomach flutters, then it flips as he pins me with his gaze.

"So . . ."

Tingles race down my body at the way he's staring at me.

Because that look in my friend's eyes? It's not coming from smack talk.

It's desire I see.

It's confirmation that the touches, the moments, the teasing weren't one-sided.

That whatever's been brewing between us is a two-way deal.

Want is written on his face, evident in his expression as Ransom cups my cheeks and whispers, "Would you like a thousand-dollar kiss?"

Do I ever.

"Yes."

He brushes his lips to mine.

My breath hitches, and my world goes *whoosh*.

7

RANSOM

I like bets.

I enjoy wagers.

And I cherish a helluva challenge.

But when I see Teagan walk backstage, I don't care that much about Martinez's smackdown.

Sure, an extra grand is nice. I won't thumb my nose at that. But the money isn't what motivates me.

It's the look in Teagan's blue eyes.

It's the confidence, mixed with her warmth. It's the determination, paired with her cleverness. It's the way she found the loophole during the auction, how she made sure we'd win the top prize.

And most of all, it's *her.*

All my reasons not to kiss her slip away from me tonight, and I'm buzzed on this evening.

On the fun we have.

I clasp her face, ask to kiss her, then I move in close.

And I *forget.*

I forget my lines.

I forget all the people milling around us, filling out forms, writing down details. All the noise and the talking. The clicking of shoes, the sound of voices, the music from the sound system.

All of that falls softly to the ground, then disappears like melting snow.

I dip my mouth to hers, almost touching.

There's *that* moment.

The movie moment.

The one right before the kiss. Where the world slows, the camera zooms in, and the audience waits.

Will he?

Won't he?

And I never thought much about those moments in flicks before. Never bought into them.

Now I get it.

Because I want to memorize every second of Teagan.

I want to remember how this *first* is going to feel.

To recall the anticipation I feel right now.

The desire coursing through my body.

The sheer intensity of my want for this woman. Right or wrong, lines or no lines, I want to kiss her so damn badly.

I savor this moment, but not as much as I savor the next, when I brush my lips over hers.

My world narrows to their softness, the taste of her gloss, and the feel of her mouth, warm and pliant.

She opens to me immediately, parts her lips. Invites me to kiss her more deeply. Asks with her body for more than a gentle, tender kiss.

Makes it clear she wants the *now* too.

As I kiss her, my head turns hazy with longing, and my body tries to insist on getting closer to her.

But somewhere in the back of my mind, I don't entirely forget we're in public.

I remember.

So I kiss her as chastely as I can, all while wanting to devour her lips. All while wishing I could consume her mouth.

Because she tastes so fucking good.

She tastes like months of pent-up desire, all sexy and snug in a violet dress with a fiery mouth and a helluva mind.

She kisses just like she talks. With spice and wit. With confidence and playfulness. She nips on my lower lip, then dusts her lips over mine before we separate.

I blink. Swallow hard.

She smiles, breathes hard, runs her tongue along her teeth.

And then the moment tips over.

She lifts her hand, runs a finger across my bow tie, and locks her eyes with mine again.

She doesn't say anything.

But her hand on my tie speaks volumes.

It says, *Let's take this off.*

In a low voice only for her, I whisper, "Do you want to get out of here?"

Her answer is immediate. "I do."

* * *

There's no choice between her place or mine—mine is closer.

Travel time is a potential buzzkill, but there's no avoiding the lull in the action. Like the seventeen-minute intermission between quarters in a hockey game, the break can sometimes be good, and sometimes be bad.

By the time Teagan and I weave through the crowd and make our way out of the Luxe, we're five minutes post-kiss.

The problem with downtime and sex is that the more seconds that pass between contact, the more chance of someone backing out.

I don't want to back out, and I hope to hell Teagan doesn't.

But I know how intermissions work.

During the break from the ice, momentum can change.

It can slip and slide.

I don't want to lose the momentum.

I want to speed up.

I want to drown myself in Teagan.

As soon as we leave the hotel, I hail a cab, and once we're inside and I give the cabbie my address, I lean across Teagan, brush away a strand of red hair that fell from her twist, and dust my lips across her cheek.

She shivers, and I confess. There's no point in pretending.

"I've wanted to kiss you for so long," I tell her as I sweep my lips along her jawline, up her neck to her ear.

She's silent for a beat, then her soft words come. "You have?"

I breathe out hard, slide a hand across her face, and pull back to meet her gaze.

"Yeah. Sometimes when we're out, I have to fight not to stare at your lips. I have to try to erase all these wild thoughts of kissing you senseless," I say as the cab whips through a yellow light at rocket speed, jerking me away from her for a second.

I tip my forehead in the direction of the driver. "I think Captain Speedy is my new best friend."

She smiles conspiratorially. "Me too. Maybe he can press turbo boost next."

I dip my head, inching closer, my lips on her cheek again. "Now, where was I?"

"Kissing me senseless?"

I hum against her soft skin, drawing a deep inhale of her strawberry shampoo. "Yes. Fuck yes. I want to get my lips on you, my hands on you."

"I'm good with both of those," she says as the driver slams the brakes at the next light, jolting us.

Laughing, I reach for her hand and link my fingers through hers. "But maybe I should behave until we get to my place."

She squeezes back, and I count off the seconds till the yellow car pulls up to my building on Park Avenue and Thirty-Sixth Street. I hand a twenty to the driver and get the hell out of the vehicle.

Inside, Oscar flashes me a grin. "How was your evening, Mr. North?"

"Fantastic, and I believe it's about to be even more fantastic," I say, racewalking past him.

Teagan waves to the guy. "Hope yours is too."

We practically fly across the lobby, and I stab the elevator button.

"C'mon, c'mon," I say.

She laughs. "Eager much?"

"Eager a lot," I answer as the doors open. Then I step inside, crowd her in a corner, and take her lips for Oscar and all of Park Avenue to see as the silver doors slide shut.

"And now I *will* kiss you senseless." I do, hard and desperate, and it's as if the kiss unlocks something inside me.

Yes, I've been attracted to Teagan King.

Yes, I've fantasized about her.

And yes, I've craved her intensely.

But I had no idea that my desire ran this deep, this far. As I kiss her, I swear it's as if I'm pouring years of longing into this kiss.

Maybe I've been waiting for this for some time now.

Perhaps it was inevitable, but I'm finally getting everything I've wanted with her.

Wanted but denied myself.

Seems she feels the same way.

She responds as if she does. Her hands slink up my chest, slide around my neck, and then she grabs me. Hard.

And holy fuck.

This is awesome.

My God, I love nothing better than a partner who wants it.

A woman who's into it.

I want the give and the take, the back and the forth.

And I'm getting that with Teagan.

I am getting it good as she takes over, kissing me fiercely, sucking on my tongue and driving me out of my mind with pleasure.

I growl as the elevator slows. "I want you so much."

Her eyes are wild. "Want you too."

In seconds, we're at my door. I unlock it, toss the keys on the entryway table, shed my jacket, and wrap my arms around her, jerking her against me.

I'm hungry for her, ravenous and needy.

But I also have so many things I want to say—things that are rising up inside me. "I kissed you tonight for you. Not for the money. You need to know that. It wasn't for a grand. It was for me. I fucking want you."

Her eyes sparkle with desire. "Good. Because I don't want fake kisses."

I push against her, letting her feel the full length of my arousal. "This feel fake?" I ask with a crooked grin.

She moans, then her lips curve into a coy smile. "No, but maybe do that again so I can be sure."

I do as she asks, grinding against her.

She sighs—a sexy, needy sound that floats across the charged air. "I want you too. But what are we doing, Ransom?"

Those words.

Those hard, heavy words.

Heavy enough to bring this night to a screeching halt.

What are we doing?

I'm doing everything I vowed I wouldn't do.

And yet . . .

"What do you want to do?" I ask, my breath coming fast as I still my hands. "Because I don't want to keep my hands off of you. But if you want me to stop, say the word and I will."

"I want all this," she says, toying with the knot on my tie. "Badly."

I lean in and steal a kiss. I savor it—the taste of her, the feel of her.

"But?" I ask as I pull back. "Because I hear a 'but' in there."

"But I don't want this to change anything," she says, then shrugs. "Which sounds stupid. Or crazy."

I smile like she's just handed me the world. "It sounds perfect." I thread my hands through her hair, letting the soft strands spill over my fingers as I meet her gaze. "Let's make a deal. Let's do this, and let's do it the right way. So it ruins nothing."

"We can do that," she says, unknotting my tie, freeing it from the collar. "We can stay friends. We can have one night."

"We absolutely can," I groan as she works open the top shirt button, and I slide my hands to the back of her dress. "We can so do this." I find the zipper and glide it down, tooth by metal tooth.

Each click of the zipper unlocking turns me on.

Each shudder from her arouses me more.

The prospect of having her the way I've wanted is driving me wild with lust. "T," I begin as she undoes another button.

"Yeah?" Her voice is dreamy, feathery.

"If I'd met you at a bar all those months ago, I'd have taken you home that night. I'd have had you naked and under me, naked and over me, naked and any way you want."

The long, sexy sigh that falls from her lips is so damn enticing.

She glances down at her clothes. "Keep going, Ransom. Because I'd have wanted that too."

Kicking the moment up ten notches, I move quickly, like this is a play on the ice and I need to get down to the net.

There's an opening, and I seize it.

I yank the zipper, driven by need, by this intense desire thrumming in my veins.

"I didn't think you were interested," she says quickly, feverishly, her fingers undoing my buttons at a frenzied pace.

I scoff. "I was interested from the moment I met you." I slide the dress off her arms, then lower the material to her waist. Drawing in a deep breath, I drink in the sight of Teagan in a pale pink bra, all lacy and see-through, revealing her nipples. Dear God, those are perfect dusky-rose nipples. "And I am very interested in taking this off you right the fuck now."

In seconds, I unhook the bra, groaning lasciviously as I free her beautiful breasts.

"The only thing that stopped me was . . ." But I can't

talk anymore, because I need my mouth full of these beauties.

Or really, one of them, because you can't truly have two boobs in your mouth at once.

Shame, that.

But there's nothing shameful about *this*.

I cup her right breast in my hand, cover her left with my mouth, and draw her nipple between my lips, kissing and sucking and licking.

There.

That works for some two-handed breast action.

Her hands move to my hair, threading through the strands. "I was interested too. So much. So damn much. I wanted you all the time."

Her words torch me. They turn me on more and more. Higher and higher. And I have got to get her naked and get inside her.

I let go of her breasts and do what I've wanted to do since the moment I met her. I scoop her up in my arms.

She laughs. "I'm half undressed," she says as I carry her across the living room to my bedroom.

"And that's a big fucking problem that I'm about to solve," I say, setting her gently on the bed, sliding off her heels.

"And *this* is a big problem, Ransom," she says, flapping her hand in my direction. "You are far too dressed."

I stand, shuck off my shirt, then undo my pants.

"Hold on," she says, sticking out a stop-sign hand.

I huff. I do not want to stop. But if I have to, I will. Obviously. "What is it, sunshine?" I ask, that term of endearment falling from my tongue automatically. I didn't plan to call her that. But it fits her. For all the shit she's been through, this woman is like the sun. She's bright and cheery, bold and outgoing, and sexier than anyone I've ever met. "You okay?"

"I'm so fucking fine," she says as she rises and strips off her dress, letting it fall to the floor. "I just want a little entertainment. I've only fantasized about getting you naked ten thousand times. Give a girl a show, please. Take your clothes off nice and slow and sexy."

And I grin like a crazy, turned-on fool.

Because I am definitely a fool to do this.

But I don't care.

Nothing has felt this good in years.

Everything else has been empty, but being with Teagan is the opposite.

I give her what she wants, taking my sweet-ass time undoing the button on my pants, sliding down the zipper, pushing the fabric over my hips.

"Oh, yeah," she says, raising both arms, doing her own appreciative dance. "Take it off. Take it all off."

I do as she says, enjoying it too, laughing as I strip to nothing.

I'm laughing, and I'm about to fuck.

It's been ages since I've felt this turned on and this happy at the same time.

This woman.

She works some kind of magic on me.

Soon, my clothes are on the floor, and I kick them aside then run a hand over the bulge in my boxer briefs, giving her the performance she craves.

She draws a sharp breath, her eyes glassy, shining

with desire. Her lips part, and her hands slide up my abs. "Ransom, please fuck me. Please fuck me now."

And I am five thousand degrees Fahrenheit.

I shed my briefs, my cock saluting her as she reaches for it and strokes me.

Shudders wrack my body from the intensity of her hands on my dick, stroking, savoring, loving it.

I close my eyes, thrusting once, twice into her hand.

I snap my eyes open, stare at her pink panties, and shake my head. "Need these off. Now."

I climb over her, push her up on my bed, and strip those panties from her. I nearly die from lust. One red landing strip leads to the promised land.

To the glistening, gorgeous promised land of this beautiful, aroused woman. "Mmm. Need to taste you, sunshine. Need to feel you on my tongue."

With a tremble, she shuffles farther up the bed, lying back on the pillows and letting her legs fall open.

"Please," she says, whimpering.

Her begging is beautiful, and I can't take another second of it.

I settle between her thighs, bury my face in her wetness, and kiss her perfect pink pussy. My eyes roll back into my head at that first intoxicating taste. I groan as I lap her up, my own sounds getting louder and louder in tandem with hers.

She lets go, her hands curling around my head, looping through my hair, as she thrusts against my face.

I lick and suck her sweetness, flicking my tongue across her clit as she arches and rocks. She fucks my face right back, seeking her pleasure.

She's as free in bed as I imagined.

Free and turned on and relishing her lust. It's thrilling to devour her as she lets go, gives in, cries out.

She holds nothing back.

She gives me her body with everything she has.

Because soon, she's curling her fingers tight around my head, wrapping her legs around my shoulders, and fucking my face till she cries out, "Oh, God, I'm coming."

Her taste floods my tongue, and I lap her up, consuming every delicious drop of her orgasm as my dick throbs, so damn eager for attention. When she's panting and shaking, I wipe a hand across my mouth and climb over her, reaching for a condom. I open it and roll it on as her eyes flicker open.

She looks buzzed and happy, and it's so damn sexy.

"You're good at that," she murmurs, then lets her gaze drift down to my dick.

"You taste spectacular," I say, moving between her legs, rubbing the head of my cock against all that slippery wetness.

Gasping, she arches up and whispers, "When I'm home alone, playing with my toys, I can come twice."

And I nearly come right then and there. From that image. That beautiful, filthy image. That gorgeous vision of Teagan knowing her own body so well she can drive herself over the edge more than once.

I swallow past the desert in my throat, then push into her. "Let's make it a double tonight, then."

Her smile is wicked. "Yes, let's."

I sink into her, pleasure gripping me every-fucking-where. She gasps, grabbing my ass and wasting no time tugging me all the way into her. She pauses for a second as I fill her, then whispers, "This is so good."

"So damn good," I agree, my cock twitching, my body sizzling. "And I want to watch you play with your toys someday."

"Want you to, Ransom. I want you to watch me sometime," she whispers.

I suppose it should worry me that we just planned another time.

That as much as we said this would be a one-off one-night, we already know we want more.

But that's just the sex talking, surely.

It's just the fantastic, mind-bending sex.

Because fucking Teagan is incredible.

It's everything I thought it would be and more.

Because she gives.

She's so free with her body, so at ease with her pleasure, that it unleashes a new wave of desire in me, over me, under me.

I want her more and more with every thrust, every snap of my hips. As I go deeper, she hooks her legs tighter around my back, digs her nails in harder. As I move, she responds, and we moan and groan together.

I don't know if it's the rhythm or the position, or if it's because this is our first time together.

But we're in sync every second, wanting each other with the same ferocity.

And that flips the switch.

In her, it seems, as she arches her back, her mouth parting.

And in me too, as I follow her to the other side, chasing her second orgasm with my first, a powerful, agonizingly blissful release that blurs the world.

When I collapse next to her, she strokes my hair, and I breathe out hard.

Words seem hard.

Nearly impossible.

But when they come, I say, "Stay the night."

And she says yes.

8

RANSOM

So.

That happened.

I should regret it, but I don't.

And I don't regret it when it happens again.

Because why screw once when you can go twice?

This time the redhead rides me, and what a view.

Her tits bounce, and her hair spills down her back, all that gorgeous flesh on display. I run my hands up and down her stomach as she goes to town on my cock.

And all I can think is fuck the mantra.

The mantra is in time-out for tonight.

When we come together, she collapses on top of me, hot, sweaty, and perfectly fucked. I brush a kiss against her silky hair, and yeah, this feels like a one-night vacation. It's twenty-four hours in the land of bliss with the woman I've wanted.

After I get rid of the condom, she slides up against me, and I stroke her hair.

"Thanks for bidding on me," I say.

"Thanks for asking me to." She turns and props her head in her hand. "So, you beat all your friends tonight. You went for the most, hottie pants."

I nod, laughing. "I sure did, thanks to you."

"Does that feel good? To have won?"

I laugh, running a hand along her hip. "Not as good as fucking you."

She rolls her eyes and shoves my shoulder. "Thanks, North. Appreciate the props."

North.

That's good, right? Sliding right back into the familiar friend zone where I'm North and she's King.

"No problem, King. Happy to give it to you anytime."

She smirks. "That's what she said."

I crack up, sliding my hand down my face. Then I flip to my side and poke her. "I thought you weren't saying that. You broke your resolution."

She shrugs. "It's not the only one I broke tonight."

That makes me curious. "Did you have a resolution not to sleep with me?"

"Well, yeah. One, I didn't think you wanted to. But we also have a gazillion friends in common, and us getting involved is one helluva bumpy ride."

"That's what she said," I mutter.

She nudges my side with her elbow. "You're just as bad as me."

"Some things are too hard to resist."

She rolls her eyes. "You are just giving me low-hanging fruit tonight, aren't you, North?"

I lift the covers, checking out my junk. "I dunno. Is it low-hanging?"

She laughs again, and it's such a great sound. Warm and welcoming. Buoyant too. "You are the worst."

I hold up a finger. "Okay, that's *not* what she said. That's definitely not what she said."

She buries her face in my neck, chuckling. "You are not allowed to make puns anymore. You're forbidden."

"Says the queen of puns and jokes. Which is awesome, because it's the opposite of . . ."

Shit. I didn't mean to say that.

She arches a brow, curious. "Opposite of what?"

I gulp and can't hide a wince. "My ex. She was very serious. Sorry. I'm an ass for mentioning her."

"Oh." It comes out heavily, and maybe I've ruined the mood.

Actually, there's no maybe about it. Mentioning an ex is a 100 percent guaranteed mood-destroyer.

"Sorry I mentioned her, King."

She quickly rearranges her features into a small smile. "It's okay. I'm not upset. Just surprised. You never mention her. So I was kind of taken aback."

"And I shouldn't have mentioned her when we're in bed. That was dumb."

"Um, hello. We're not banging. It's okay to talk. Was it a bad breakup?"

I sigh. "On a scale of one to nuclear, it was the atom bomb."

She frowns, running a hand down my arm. "I'm sorry. That sucks."

I shake my head. "Listen, we don't have to talk about exes in bed."

"I know we don't. But it doesn't bother me either. My last relationship went nuclear too."

Oh? "It did?"

She swallows, then speaks. "We'd been together for a few years. We were pretty serious—lived together and all. I was with him when my dad died. And I was pretty devastated."

"As well you should be. That's completely understandable. But what happened?" I ask, bracing myself for her pain.

"He couldn't handle it. He couldn't handle my grief. He said it was too much for him." Her voice is tense, her eyes a little shiny.

Shock tightens my muscles. "He wasn't there for you during one of the hardest things you'd ever gone through? He couldn't man up and support you?"

"Exactly," she says, taking a deep breath. "He left me. Said he couldn't deal with it."

"Jesus," I say with a heavy sigh. "And I thought I'd been dealt a shit hand."

She meets my gaze, her eyes soft. "What happened?"

This should be hard to say. I don't like to talk about Edie. When I say her name, my body tenses. Only this time, nothing hurts. It's remarkably easy to speak the truth to Teagan. "She was my best friend. She was my girlfriend. She was the woman I thought I'd marry and have kids with. A little over two years ago, I planned a romantic night out. I had a ring. I took her to dinner. And when I was about to ask her to marry me, she told me she'd fallen in love with someone else."

It feels better than I thought it would to get those

words out. The war wound doesn't ache like it has every other time before.

The words don't resurrect the old pain.

This time, it's simply a story and not a fresh serving of heartache.

Still, Teagan's hand flies to her mouth. "My God. That's awful."

"It kind of sucked," I say. That's the goddamn truth, even if I don't ache like I used to.

She runs her hand down my arm again. "That's an understatement, Ransom. That's terrible."

"And so is what happened with your ex. But listen, I'm not in love with her. I'm not sad anymore. I'm all good." And I mean it—every word. I'm officially all good in bed with this fantastic woman. But it also feels nice to say to her, to let her in.

Teagan gives a faint smile. "We officially have some of the best worst-ex sob stories."

I laugh lightly. "We sure do."

As she jokes, something occurs to me. Teagan's incredibly good at teasing. At keeping things light. I tilt my head and meet her gaze, zeroing in on a hunch. "Is this why you're funny? Why you like to have a good time?"

"Because of my ex?"

"Because of your ex. Because of losing your family. Because you've been through some serious hell. Is it your way of coping?"

She studies the white linen of the sheet, running her hand over the seam, but she doesn't tell me to back off or stop questioning.

So, I don't. "They say humor gets you through grief. And look, I'm not trying to co-opt what you went through. But I was pretty shaken after Edie left me, and it was when Martinez took me to some comedy clubs that I started feeling human again."

Teagan grins, a sweet, delighted smile. "He did that? The guy you trash-talk?"

"He and Carnale. They knew I wasn't happy. They wanted to cheer me up."

"Did it work?"

I flash back on those nights when two of my peeps showed up at my door, insisted I get my ass off the couch, and then took me out to have a good time. They knew I didn't need a strip club or a bar. I needed some deep belly chuckles. "Yeah, it did. And I'm happy again," I say, wrapping up the tale. "Smarter now. More careful. But humor got me through. Is that what did it for you?"

She nods slowly, as if considering it fully, then says, "I think so—laughter as an antidote to pain. If you can laugh when you're grieving, it's wonderful medicine. That got me through, and so did my friendship with Bryn."

"Yeah? She helped you?" I ask.

"She lost her mom and had a shitty situation with her ex too, so we met in grief support and bonded over both of those things. Then we wound up working together. She got me the job at The Dating Pool."

I park my hands behind my head, relaxing even more, smiling as she lets me deeper into her life. It makes me happy that Teagan has someone like Bryn to rely on. Someone who's there for her, and vice versa.

"That's awesome that you're so close—that you worked together and are also such great friends."

"She's a terrific friend. Like a sister, in a way. I was actually talking to her when you were backstage. Before everything started with the auction," she says, and there's a flash of something—insecurity, maybe—in her eyes.

"What did you talk to her about?" I ask, curious what's going on in her head.

She waves airily as she brushes some strands of hair off her cheek. "Oh, just the whole thing. Would I ever possibly be able to bid enough? That kind of thing." She goes all dramatic, and I feel like she's disguising something, but I'm not sure what.

"And did she say just go for it? Bet big on the stud?" I ask, opting for humor too. But it doesn't feel as right as it usually does. Almost like, after the conversations we've had tonight, we can't just revert back to surface-level, to banter without depth.

But it's not only that we've shared stories that makes the usual verbal fun and games unsatisfying.

It's the other part.

Being in bed with her.

Wanting to be in bed with her again.

And knowing it's a bad idea.

She taps my shoulder. "Yes, she encouraged me to bet everything on the hockey stud we're all buddies with."

That's why we're a bad idea. "Yeah, the whole lot of us. Our crazy, tangled pack of friends."

"We're lucky. Damn lucky to have great friends." I

offer her a fist for knocking, and she knocks back. And hell, I'm grateful to have Teagan in that pack, and I don't want to lose her either.

I yawn, and since yawns are contagious, she serves one up right after me. I wrap an arm around her. "One night of snuggling?"

"Definitely. It won't change a thing," she says, repeating our vow from earlier.

"No way. We've got this," I say, bringing her a little bit closer, holding her a tiny smidge tighter.

This won't change a thing.

9

TEAGAN

We got this.

When I wake up the next morning next to a still-sleeping Ransom, I reach for my phone out of habit. A message flashes across the screen—a text from Bryn.

When I slide it open, I smile.

It's a group text, and Ransom has already responded, so he must have woken up long enough to read it and reply.

Bryn: Brunch today? Fox and Gavel. Yes, it's one of those ultra-trendy brunch spots, but Dean knows the owner and got us in, and the French toast is supposed to be divine. See you at noon. Be there or else.

Like a slot machine payout, the group thread is bursting with replies.

Fitz: Obviously, we will be there.

Logan: Hey, Bryn, since you're right next to me, you know I'm going. But this is me, chiming in anyway.

Oliver: Aww, aren't you cute with your bedside chime-ins. I'll be there. So will your sister, Logan. There, I chimed in for her.

Summer: Hey! I can speak for myself. I'll be there.

The last text in the thread makes my heart glow.

Ransom: I'm in.

It's just a reply. Nothing special. But seeing that it flew across the internet at five forty-five a.m. tells me something. Ransom woke, saw the invitation, and answered it while I was asleep, knowing he'd want to go to brunch with our friends—and, potentially, me.

And now it's my turn, and I write back with my official RSVP.

Teagan: Divine French toast is calling my name.

There. Done.

That was surprisingly easy—all of it.

Sex. Talking. Sleeping.

Then returning to normal.

Staying part of the crew.

Scrolling through my Instagram feed, I replay the simplicity of all those things, as I lie here in bed with a sleeping sports star next to me.

Wait. Forget Instagram.

The live view is way better. I'll just ogle Ransom for a bit. Yup, I'm a perv, but no one can blame me.

Because . . .

His carved pecs. His sculpted abs. His most excellent ass, courtesy of the NHL. Thank you, hockey, for giving him a great butt.

That butt was fantastic to hold on to last night while he fucked me.

I shiver as the memory rushes through me. It feels like a dream. An intense, fevered one, but a dream nonetheless.

Three orgasms.

Then a long, deep conversation, filled with laughter and truths.

And it wasn't weird.

Neither of us wants anything more than this—the utter simplicity of waking up next to someone who gets you and who doesn't ask anything more of you.

Who won't hurt you.

Who won't take away the things you love.

A small yawn escapes my lips, and I wince.

Because . . . morning breath.

That is not acceptable.

No way can I let Ransom smell me in the morning. I wriggle around him, sliding toward the end of the bed and quietly swinging my feet to the floor.

I pad across the hardwood to the bathroom, shutting the door and locking it.

Whew.

Inside his very manly bathroom—where it's all chrome and white, ocean-spice deodorant, black bottles of shampoo, and manly lotions and potions—I pee then track down some mouthwash. As I gargle, I hunt for toothpaste then scrub with my finger like a toothbrush.

I exhale, breathing a sigh of relief.

There. Fresh as a daisy.

When I turn around to reach for a hand towel, my gaze snags on a shelf of toiletries—including a mint-green stick of deodorant. Spring lavender. My brow knits. Next to it is body lotion. Vanilla honey. And a hairbrush.

My throat tightens, and my chest convulses.

These are for women.

Are they for hookups?

He is known for enjoying the ladies, and there's nothing wrong with that, since he's single.

Wait, *is* he single? These things—the lotion, the brush—belong to someone. Is he seeing someone *and* fucking me?

My stomach recoils.

A wave of panic rolls over me.

When I leave the bathroom, my shoulders are tight and my pulse is racing with the hope that he's still asleep.

I need to get out of here. I need to let go of these warm, fuzzy feelings and return to some kind of normal before our brunch.

I gather my clothes, head to his living room, then get dressed in record time. With my shoes in hand, I tiptoe to the door, unlatching it.

"Hey, you."

I wince.

"Hi." It sounds icy. I try again, injecting some warmth in my tone. "Hi there."

I turn around to find the gorgeous man clad only in black boxer briefs. He's scratching his jaw. "Hmm. Looks like you were making a dine and dash."

Against my better judgment, a laugh bursts from me. I collect myself, trying to go for a cool and casual vibe. "I just need to go. Stuff to do before . . ."

Yeah, this isn't working as well as I thought, and he knows it.

He arches a skeptical brow. "Before brunch with our friends?"

I slap on a smile, my brain whirring through plausible activities that would send me skedaddling. "Yes. I have this shelf I wanted to organize. Plants to water. And I have to pick up . . . popcorn." What a horrible, terrible liar I am.

"Wouldn't want to get in the way of you buying popcorn," he says dryly.

"It's to take to work tomorrow," I improvise. "Snacks for the meeting."

"Super important, snack time is."

"But hey," I say, fixing on a smile, oh-so-happy. "Thanks for last night." I plaster on my farewell grin when it threatens to slip. "It was super awesome. And now I should go. I'll see you at brunch, and it'll be fab."

"Teagan," he says warily.

"Yes?" It comes out chipper. Too chipper.

His eyes narrow, not with distrust, but with concern. "Are you okay? Because you don't seem okay."

I square my shoulders. I need to get out of here—my chest is tight with holding back my questions. I desperately want to quiz Ransom on his bathroom, but that is so not chill. That's not what a friend would do. It's what a girlfriend would do, and I'm not and won't ever be his girlfriend. "I'm so good. I'm all good."

"And yet you just thanks-for-last-night-ed me."

"Right," I say, keeping my cool as best I can. "Because we agreed to one night. It all goes back to normal today. So, this is me being totally normal."

I don't sound normal at all.

He walks over to me, slides a hand around my waist, and drops his lips to mine. He kisses me, soft and sweet and minty fresh. He must have slipped out of bed and brushed his teeth while I was gathering my clothes.

Something about him wanting fresh breath both bothers me and turns me on. Like I'm just part of his routine with women.

And like he also wanted to kiss me again.

The first is irrational, I know, since I did the exact same thing. But that was before the vanilla honey and the hairbrush, and now it makes me furious to think he has a routine with women—brush teeth, check; kiss good morning, check—and I'm just part of his habit.

But I like that he wanted to kiss me again. It turns me on for all the reasons racing through my head: He tastes so good. He feels amazing. His kisses make my bones sing and my blood hum. They make my heart pound fast.

I like kissing Ransom too much.

I like *him* too much.

And I don't know how to snap back to friendship. All I know is I have to try because friends don't leave on a sour note.

I slide a hand up his bare chest, and *ohhh* . . .

That doesn't help.

His muscles are so defined, so firm, so delicious. He's like a sculpture come to life. Touching him sends me to a hazy, buzzy feel-good world. But it's not a world I can live in.

I stop the path of my hand, taking a breath, and I woman up. "Why do you have spring lavender deodorant in your bathroom?"

He screws up the corner of his lips. "Huh?"

"And vanilla-honey lotion. And a hairbrush. Are you seeing someone?"

A chuckle bursts from him. Loud and boisterous. And far too amused. He wraps an arm around me and yanks me close, tucking a finger under my chin. "Yes.

Every Saturday, my sister comes over. She showers between shows."

I shake my head. That doesn't compute. "What do you mean?"

"She signs. For *Hamilton*. It's kind of hot in the theater, and when you're interpreting, you use your whole body. It's a workout. She likes to freshen up for the evening performance. This is close to the theater district, and she's in Brooklyn. Hence, her stuff is here." He can't stop grinning, and I can't stop a grimace, or from feeling foolish.

I am the worst. Slap on a sign and dog-shame me.

I JUMP TO CONCLUSIONS.

"Shoot. I'm sorry. I feel like an ass." I might as well be six inches tall, that's how low I feel.

Tilting my chin back up, he makes me look at him, still smirking. "Your jealousy is the cutest thing ever."

"Ugh. Pretend I never said anything. It was wildly inappropriate."

"It was wildly adorable," he says, then his expression goes serious. "But also a little insulting. I would never cheat. Never sleep with someone else while I'm seeing you." He blinks, like he just realized what he said. "I mean . . . while we're together." But that doesn't seem to be the correction he wanted either. He flubs his lips, giving up the search for the right cover-up. "You know what I mean."

"I do," I say quickly. But I don't. I don't know what either of us means or wants. I don't know why he said anything about seeing me or being together.

All I know is he looks flustered, and I insulted him,

and clearly, neither of us entirely knows how to act around the other.

But I'm the one who tried to sneak out. I'm the one who ginned up tales of plants to water and popcorn to purchase. "I'm sorry. I didn't mean to suggest you'd do that. That was terrible. And I'm not even sure why it upset me. I think . . . I just saw those toiletries, and I felt . . . silly. Can we please rewind? Go back to an hour ago when I was chill?"

He takes a moment to consider it, then nods. "You're chill. We're chill. It's all good. Like we said last night, right?"

"It's so good."

"But you need to know I could tell you were upset. Want to know how?"

"How?"

"Because you kept trying to joke. And after what we talked about last night, I started thinking maybe that wasn't just about you trying to be lighthearted. That maybe you were covering up something that hurt."

Damn him. He's too observant. Or maybe I let him in too far. If he can see that about me, he can hurt me, like my ex did. The wounds aren't fresh, but the scars last forever.

But even with the scars, a part of me likes that he understood how I was feeling, maybe even before I did.

"I was a little upset."

"And now? Do you feel better?"

A small smile tugs at my lips. "I do."

He drops a kiss onto my forehead, sweet and tender.

More tender than I deserve. "Good. I don't want to hurt you," he whispers.

His words float across my skin like a warm breeze in the summer. "I don't want to hurt you either."

"Then let's keep *not* hurting each other." He steps back, lifts his hands, then signs something. I have no idea what he's saying.

I shrug, confused. "Help a girl out?"

He slows it down, repeating the finger moves as he says, "I said, *It's all good.*"

I smile. "I like that. I'm glad you said that."

He signs again, then says, "Anytime."

After a goodbye, I leave, but I don't feel all good.

Because a part of me wishes I were staying.

Wishes I were getting ready at his place.

Leaving with him.

That we were going to brunch together.

But that's not going to happen.

* * *

When I arrive at the West Village sidewalk café, the whole crew is draped over chairs, shades on, laughing, chatting.

Bryn waves broadly then stands and gives me a hug, whispering, "Tell me everything about last night."

I shake my head, mouthing *Later* and wondering if she can tell that Ransom and I slept together. Whether it's written in my eyes, or she simply has best-friend X-ray vision. Likely that last one.

Logan stands too, his brown eyes twinkling. "Good to see you, Teagan. What's the report?"

"You were there, goading us. You should know," I say with a sassy stare.

"But I wasn't there," Summer says. "Did he cost five bucks or ten?"

"Did you use a coupon to save some money?" Bryn chimes in. "Or maybe a promo code?"

"They don't have promo codes for something that cheap," Summer says.

"I *was* a prize last night, assholes," Ransom says, flipping them the bird.

"I bet you were a prize. Like the kind at the bottom of a cereal box," Oliver teases.

"And she won me for a fuck ton of money."

Fitz pats his chest. "Thanks to us making sure you went for the most."

"Thanks, I think," Ransom says.

"Now tell us," Dean says, lifting his tea, likely English breakfast, "where will you go on this special date? Statue of Liberty? Empire State Building?"

Fitz laughs then drapes an arm around his fiancé. "I told you I'd take you to those places, babe."

"You've been telling me that for months. Still haven't made it," Dean remarks, lifting a brow.

"Seems you're just too busy," Summer says, smirking at the two guys getting married next weekend.

Bryn laughs, a wink in her tone as she says, "Nothing wrong with busy."

Then all my friends raise their mugs, lifting their coffees and teas high and clinking.

Toasting to being too busy.

Because they *are* too busy. With each other. With love. With being together.

My heart squeezes like someone's hugging it. This is what I love. This is what I need.

These people. This gorgeous image of my newfound family.

Not another round of hot sex.

And not hot sex that gets ruined by my own strange bloom of feelings.

Because hot sex and blooming feelings can destroy this second chance at happiness that I have with my friends.

When I look at Ransom and he flashes a friendly smile at me, I'm sure he must be thinking the same: *Thank God we didn't blow this by wanting more than we should have.*

Because showing up here as the brand-new couple —the couple that will never stick because we aren't serious people and neither one of us wants a lasting thing—would snarl this ball of yarn that we both need.

Love might work for these other people.

But for people like us? It's not in the cards.

After we order, the conversation returns to the auction, and Fitz clears his throat, his eyes locking with mine as he gestures to Ransom. "So, you won our guy. Well done. We knew Ransom would be the prize cat and beat out Carnale and Martinez."

I blow on my fingernails. "Meow indeed."

Oliver runs a hand across the back of his neck and

tilts his head. "Question though. Who won the Yankees closer?"

"I can only presume his grandma was phoning in a bid," Fitz chimes in, then nods to Ransom. "Sound about right?"

I laugh. "No doubt. Or maybe one of his cats."

"Puss? Boots?" Ransom offers. "Or Puss, backed by Boots?"

We laugh, then proceed to guess who might have been angling for the closer, and I'm grateful that Ransom and I can talk like this, sliding right back into the crew on the morning after a night like the one the two of us had.

Even though this brunch hurts my heart a bit more than I expected.

Because when the meal ends, everyone else goes home together, arm in arm, holding hands.

Ransom and I go home in opposite directions, alone.

Last night truly was a one-time thing.

I need to remember that last night was a hookup—one with a friend I care about but still a one-off—especially when Bryn messages me several hours later, demanding all the details from the auction.

Bryn: About that *later*. It's later now, and I want details, and I'm pretty sure the details are going to be my favorite kind—*dirty*.

Teagan: Ah, yes, you do love that variety.

Bryn: I do, and therefore . . . gimme, gimme, gimme.

I'm dying to clutch a pillow, tuck into my couch, and serve it up with a glass of wine and a side dish of girl talk. But it's best to keep the convo simple, since that's how I'm keeping things with Ransom.

Teagan: In a nutshell, we got it out of our systems, and we're back to normal.

Bryn: Out of your systems? Has anyone ever wanted less sex after having good sex? It was good sex, right?

When I don't answer immediately, Bryn calls me two seconds later.

"Spill."

I laugh as I empty my dishwasher, setting plates in the cupboard. "We went home together. We slept together. We agreed it wouldn't change a thing."

She squeals. "How was it?"

"Amazing." My chest flips as I remember how it felt to be with him.

"Did you just sigh?"

"No! That was not a sigh!" I say, denying, denying, and then denying some more.

"So it wasn't sigh-worthy?"

It was song-worthy, album-worthy, skywriter-worthy.

And while a lady doesn't kiss and tell, Bryn and I tell each other everything. Also, I know there's a good chance the gist of this will get back to Logan, and I would never do Ransom the disservice of selling him short. Especially since there is nothing short about Ransom.

"It was amazing, as in multiples, as in insert adjectives like toe-curling and sheet-grabbing," I say as she squeals like we're both curled up on the couch clutching our pillows. But I try to tell the story matter-of-factly. "And I slept over too. And the best part is, brunch proves that we did all that banging and it doesn't have to change a thing," I say, focusing on the deal Ransom and I made, adding a cheery grin for good measure as I slide a glass to the back of the cupboard.

Bryn chuckles. "You said he rocked your world. That is the literal definition of changing things."

"I mean it won't change a thing today. In the daytime. Not in bed," I say, sticking to logic.

"But why?"

"Because we won't let it. We don't want it to," I say.

"At the risk of sounding like a Netflix glitch . . . BUT WHY?"

"You know why," I say as I finish with the dish-washer, then hunt in my fridge for something to cook for dinner. Maybe eggs and mushrooms? That is the decision of the moment, and I focus on it. The question of more than one night with Ransom is not up for debate.

The sympathy in Bryn's sigh puts my back up. But not literally, because my head is inside the fridge. "You truly don't want to even consider a relationship?"

I bristle at the idea. "Relationships have the potential to destroy your soul." I find the mushrooms and grab a cutting board. "And I don't want to ruin my friendship with him, and especially not the chemistry with our friends. Which is why it's perfect that he's not interested in anything more, and neither am I. You know that."

She huffs. "You guys say that now . . ."

I shake my head, amused, as I wash the veggies then line them up to slice. "We say it now because it's true."

"It might not always be true," she points out.

"It's true enough for me," I say, then segue to the topic of Fitz and Dean's wedding next weekend.

When I end the call and whip up the omelet, I repeat the words to myself. It is true.

True enough.

Because otherwise, I'll want a man I shouldn't have.

A relationship that might rattle and rock all I hold near and dear—my found family.

But when I finish dinner, clean up, and walk through my empty apartment, I miss him already.

So much more than I expected.

10

RANSOM

Luna arches a dubious brow as she mixes a cocktail. It's her *is this a true story* look as I recount the tale of the auction.

Tempest laughs, nodding, then answers her in sign language. "It's true. Someone actually wants to date him." My sassy sister—well, one of them—finishes by pointing her thumb at me.

"Stranger things have happened," Luna says. She *can* speak, but she prefers to sign. She also prefers to make the drinks, since she says we suck at mixing cocktails, which is why her speedy hands are occupied.

From my spot on a barstool, I roll my eyes as Luna adds mint to the mojitos. We're at her apartment, and her husband is picking up takeout Thai food.

"I was the prize last night, ladies. I went for the highest donation, and that donation goes to the companion dog organization," I say with my hands, gesturing to the big blonde Labrador sprawled on the floor.

Angela raises her snout at the word and the sign for "dog," since she knows both. "Yes, you, girl," I say to the gentle beast. "I'm talking about you."

Luna puts down the glasses, rounds the bar to me, and wraps me in a hug, her blonde curls smushed against my face. When she lets go, she meets my gaze and says, "Thank you."

"My pleasure," I say, making sure she can read my lips.

She returns to her mixing, and I continue the conversation by hand. "Admit it. I'm irresistible."

They both laugh, then Luna signs, "In his mind, he's a legend. So, who is this woman who bought you?"

"Yes, tell us everything about the miracle of last night," Tempest adds.

Miracle.

I laugh privately. Sex with Teagan was like a miracle of pleasure. It was a revelation of bliss.

"She's great. Teagan's a friend of mine," I explain.

"And will she stay a friend?" Luna asks.

"I thought you didn't date friends?" Tempest asks.

Ah, they know me so well. "I don't date friends, and I don't plan on dating her," I say and sign, but the second those words make landfall, they feel a little off, a lot wrong.

I'd like to date Teagan.

I'd like to see her.

But that's not what we agreed to last night. We made a deal to do sex the right way, so it wouldn't ruin anything. So we'd snap back like a friendship-shaped rubber band.

Luna hands me a drink, then one to Tempest too. "But you have a date with her," Luna points out. "She won a date with you."

Tempest clears her throat, eyebrows pinching together. "Doesn't that mean you're dating?"

I suppose that's somewhat true. But not entirely. "It's just a date. That's all."

Luna arches a dubious brow. "Just a date with the woman you're always telling us about?"

I blanch, then blink. "I'm always telling you about her?"

Tempest drapes an arm around me, nodding vigorously. *Always*, she mouths.

Huh.

That sort of surprises me.

And sort of doesn't too.

"Want to hear something funny?"

They both nod.

I tell them about how Teagan was jealous of Tempest's hairbrush, thinking they'll get a kick out of the story.

And they do.

Oh hell, do they ever.

They're both howling with laughter.

So hard that I realize it's partly at me—because I pretty much unwittingly admitted that Teagan spent the night. And they seem to be laughing both at the story and at what they think it means that I'm telling them.

"As I said, you're always talking about her," Luna signs.

"Good luck with your *just a date*," Tempest adds, injecting sarcasm into her fingers.

It's something sisters are particularly good at.

11

TEAGAN

This is what going back to friendship looks like after a night of toe-curling, bone-rattling sex.

It looks like text messages to plan our charity auction smile-for-the-camera date.

As I exit the subway by The Dating Pool offices on the way to work later that week, my phone buzzes.

I wish I didn't feel a little flip in my belly when I see Ransom's name.

But I do feel it, that same zing and zip that raced through me the other morning at his place. The wish for more. A more that won't happen, so I slip into my good-time-gal persona, the one I live in nearly every second, and I read his note.

Ransom: Since a carriage ride is out, I think we should try metal-detecting on the Jersey shore for our big date.

Teagan: Yes, that's what I paid top dollar for. Let's hunt for pennies and tin.

Ransom: Fine, we'll eat Mentos and pour Diet Coke in our mouths and be human fountains. And we will do it in Times Square.

Teagan: Wow. Have you been reading my diary? Just dying to do a mouth fountain. You really know how to show a girl a good time.

Ransom: Ahem. I believe you *had* a good time.

Teagan: Correction. I had *three* good times.

Ransom: *thumps chest*

Teagan: As you should. Back to dates though, we could go rope climbing.

Ransom: We could do other things with ropes . . .

Teagan: Gee, it feels like your brain is descending into dirty territory.

Ransom: Admittedly, it spends a lot of time there. But I'll behave. I say we go to the planetarium, watch a sunset, drink milkshakes, or go to the Museum of Natural History.

Teagan: That. All of that. It sounds perfect.

Ransom: Whoa. You have a big date appetite.

Teagan: Don't be making fun of my appetite. You just dangled a ton of good stuff in front of me. I'm going to eat it all.

Ransom: That's what she said.

Teagan: *groans*

Ransom: You kind of walked into it.

Teagan: And now I must walk into work. After I pop into a bakery and get treats for the editors. It's snack time.

Ransom: Don't forget, they like popcorn too. Just saying.

I laugh at the way he busts me once more for my attempted Sunday morning exodus.

Teagan: They love it.

* * *

When I head into The Dating Pool offices, I swing my gaze to Bryn's once-upon-a-time office. She left The

Dating Pool more than a year ago, but I still miss her sometimes. Working with your best friend can be terrible or wonderful. With Bryn, it was a blast, and I long for the hallway run-ins and impromptu ladies' room conferences we used to have.

Fortunately, I love the editors and writers who are still here, so when it's time for the weekly meeting, I bring in the supplies.

"Snack time at the zoo," I declare as I set a plate of cookies on the conference table, right next to a red bowl of popcorn with *Please, sir, I want some more* printed on the inside bottom of the bowl—a gift for me from Bryn when she left.

A little piece of her at the editorial meetings.

"Thank God. I'm ravenous," says Matthew, the site's main editor, as he grabs a cookie and feasts on it. Matthew took over the content when Bryn left.

The others devour the treats as we discuss articles, posts, and columns for the site.

Rosario wiggles her hand. "I have a hella hot idea. There's an article, or a series, really, that I've been dying to do."

"Tell us what's on your mind," Matthew says, tapping on his iPad, taking notes.

"We should do a piece on married couples. Dates to keep the spark alive. That's one of our most searched for terms—fun dates for married couples."

My social media ears prick. "I love that. It's very shareable and very photographable too. Which is important."

"But we would need a married writer to do it,"

Matthew points out, screwing up his lips like he's deep in thought. "We'd need to farm it out, since none of us are hitched yet."

A buzzer beeps in my head. I know who would be perfect. "What about Summer and Oliver Harris? She's a friend of mine, and she and her husband are always trying to go on fun dates. She submitted a letter a couple of years ago for a contest on letters to your ex, so I don't know if that's an issue or a conflict of interest."

"I remember that letter. It was fantastic." Matthew taps away on his laptop, humming, then exhaling. "We never ran her piece, since there were some issues with her engagement at the time, but now that she's actually married to him after all—yay, happy endings—it wouldn't be a problem. Would she do it? She was a captivating writer."

"I'll send her a text right now." I grab my phone and fire off a message to Summer.

A minute later, her yes arrives.

"She's in," I say with a smile.

Matthew pumps a fist. Rosario holds up a hand for high-fiving. The others cheer.

"Way to go, woman!" Matthew says, and then wags a finger at me. "Now, admit it. You have a whole contact list of friends you can call on for nearly every sitch, right?"

"I do indeed," I say with a wink.

And that's how I want my life.

Busy with buddies. This weekend I'm going to Fitz's wedding with Bryn and Logan. Then I'll check out dinosaurs with Ransom for our official date. Maybe during the week, I'll go for a run with Summer.

Good times, good people, and a good life.

The life I carved out for myself after my father died. One I've worked hard to maintain and won't jeopardize.

* * *

Except, when I go home that night, I'm a little lonelier than I was before. I click open my text app, contemplating sending Ransom a text, since I desperately want to chat with him.

To trade more silly date ideas.

To send goofy gifs.

Or to just . . . talk.

Like we did on the way to the auction. Or in bed Saturday night. Or on Sunday morning too, when he saw through me to what made me tick.

When I flop down on my couch, I open the message thread with Ransom, just as a Google Alert pops up.

It's for City Post's hottest athletes.

That's interesting. Looks like this list was posted right after the auction.

I click on the piece, and I grin—Ransom's at the top, followed by Adrian, followed by the Yankees shortstop. There's an asterisk at the bottom lamenting Fitz's absence from the list.

*After several years owning these lists, James Fitzgerald is no longer eligible on account of his pending marriage to Dean Collins this weekend. Fitz, we wish you and your husband-to-be all the best for a long and happy life together, and we

thank you for all the times you did qualify for our hottest single athletes in the city.

Naturally, I screenshot that and send it to Fitz.

Teagan: I guess all good things come to an end.

Fitz: It is indeed the end of an era. And I am all good with that.

Teagan: As you should be. Quite a run while it lasted though, King of the Hotties. Former King, I mean.

Fitz: I humbly surrender my crown to the next crop of single AF jocks.

Teagan: And there are plenty of them! See you this weekend. I hear the cake is going to be dope. As well as the grooms.

Fitz: So dope that you should dance with the forward from my team. And on that note, I'm outta here!

Teagan: Good night, Cupid Groom.

I return to the thread with Ransom because I know he'll want to see this, then maybe we'll have some friendly banter over it, but that's all it will be. I'm not texting him just to text him, like a girlfriend would do. It's exactly the same as I just texted Fitz.

Teagan: Look who's on top!

Ransom: Those damn lists.

I stare at his response quizzically. It's not quite as exuberant as I'd have thought.

Teagan: You're probably tired of those. A dime a dozen.

Ransom: That's not it . . .

My phone rings, and it's the man of the hour. "Hey," he says.

"Hi. You okay?"

He doesn't answer right away, just exhales. "So, the thing is . . ."

"What's wrong?" I ask, concerned.

"Nothing. I swear it's nothing." He sighs. "How are you?"

It's not nothing. It's definitely something. "You're changing the subject. Are you sure it's nothing?"

He seems to wave it off, dismiss it, with "It's stupid."

My brow knits. "Is it though? It sounds like you're bothered. Did I touch a nerve when I sent you that list?" I ask, a little worried, since something is clearly eating at him.

"Okay, here goes. When I first started dating Edie, I was on a couple of those lists of athletes." He sounds sheepish at first, like he's embarrassed, but it's a cute sort of embarrassment. "Until the media figured out I wasn't available, and then I wasn't on them anymore." He sounds more serious than I'm used to hearing him. "But she didn't like that I *had* been on them."

I sit up straighter, listening intently. "Was she worried she'd lose you? Is that why she didn't want to see you on the single-in-the-city lists?"

"That's what I thought at first," he says heavily, like this is a painful admission. Like it costs him something to have this conversation. But he hasn't shut it down, so maybe it's a price he wants to pay.

"I take it that wasn't the reason she disliked them?"

"She had a different one."

"Do you want to tell me?" I ask gently. It sounds like he does, but he's still holding back for some reason.

"Yeah. I do." He draws a breath, and it sounds like it fuels him to continue. "See, when I first started out in the pros, the guys and me, we did the whole smack-talk thing. Which we still do, but that's when it started. We were always competing any way we could," he says, with the once-upon-a-time note of settling in to tell a story.

"Martinez and I were in different sports, but we ripped on each other about who was first in our respective drafts, who had better stats, who got on those lists and where we placed, and so on. That might sound dumb, but that's what we did. We still do. That's our currency. Hell, I do that with Fitz."

"Smack talk," I say, nodding, understanding him. "I get that."

"You do?" He sounds wildly relieved.

"I do. It's sort of like jokes. It's how you communicate. Your insults, your put-downs—they aren't truly insults. It's because you like each other. The gibes show you care, and that you're part of the group, right?"

The longest exhale of tension comes from the other end of the phone line. "Yes. *That.* Exactly."

"And she didn't like you smack-talking each other?"

"She hated it. Couldn't stand it. She despised that I texted them. That we found things to give each other a hard time about."

I laugh, a little incredulous. "Basically, she hated the things that made you, you."

He chuckles lightly, then returns to his more introspective side. "In a way, I suppose she did. She didn't entirely get it. Or get it at all." He takes a beat, then marches forward, and I wish I could see his face, but I imagine his hazel eyes are resolute, confident. "And you know what? I actually liked being on the lists again when we split. I liked it for a bunch of reasons."

"Tell me why." I want to know, and he sure seems eager to share. Maybe he's even pacing around his place now, energized.

"Because it meant I was single and wasn't being lied to anymore about how she felt. I was free from someone who didn't feel the same way I did. But most of all, because it meant I could do those things I'd missed—talk to my buddies in the way we liked to talk, hang with them—and I didn't have to worry about what she thought."

His answer makes perfect sense. And it reveals another layer to him, one I find fascinating. Men and women can present such simple fronts to the world, but behind those are so many more sides than we expect.

That's what I've learned about Ransom every time we've talked recently. I've seen his family side, his giving heart, his wounded soul, and now the guy who likes to hang with his buds—because they matter to him. Even if it seems like all they do is engage in bro banter, it's bro banter with a purpose.

And that's all kinds of cool in my book.

"Sometimes a joke is just a joke, but sometimes it's a connection to a friend," I say.

"Yes! God, yes," he says, punctuating his relief with a laugh.

"And whoever you're with should understand that your relationships with them are important to you. We shouldn't try to dictate every single behavior. We have to give the people we care about space to be themselves."

I can sense his smile as he speaks. "You get it, T. You get me."

"I try," I say, my heart glowing in my chest.

"You do more than try, Teagan," he says, then swings back to the topic. "And I still like being on the lists, but not because I care about something arbitrary like looks or a hotness meter. Whatever. I can't control that, and it truly makes no difference in my daily life. But it's this thing the guys and me bond over, even if we're insulting each other."

"Because they aren't truly put-downs," I say, a wide smile spreading across my face as he shares this glimpse of his soft, vulnerable underbelly. Who would have thought it'd be lined in insults? Yet it is.

"Don't get me wrong. Martinez is an ugly son of a bitch."

I crack up. "And all straight women in New York would disagree."

He growls. "Don't say that."

"I speak the truth." A grin spreads across my face when I add, "But I happen to think a certain hockey player is much sexier."

He hums, low and sexy. "Best. Response. Ever."

"But I get that you'd want to rib him about being number one on a single-in-the-city list."

"You definitely don't think it's weird?"

I shake my head, still grinning as I snuggle deeper into the couch. "No. I think it's cool."

He lets out another contented sigh. "I have a brilliant idea, Teagan."

"I love brilliant ideas. Lay it on me."

"Do you want to hang at Fitz's wedding this weekend?"

"Obviously," I say, and I bet he means as friends, but the invitation feels a little bit like a date too.

Or maybe it feels a lot like one.

And I like it.

12

TEAGAN

I take a half-day on Friday, powering through the morning with a flurry of scheduled posts of articles, lists, and tips we've run this past week and want to highlight again.

That includes a popular column on Made Connections, a relatively new dating app that's been taking the scene by storm, since it lets strangers post about someone interesting they've seen in passing, or perhaps met briefly but never exchanged numbers with, like Bryn and Logan, who got together exactly that way.

Our site runs a weekly story about couples who've met through the app. A guy and a gal who spotted each other on the Whole Foods escalator, one going up, the other going down. A man who chatted with a woman in yoga class, exchanging tips on meditation and wine, only to be interrupted by a fire drill. A painfully shy UPS driver who crushed so hard on a regular customer but couldn't bring himself to ask her out till he got on the app.

He's still shy, but that's okay. He found his person—and he said falling in love taught him he didn't have to be shy about expressing his heart to her.

Talk about swooning.

Their story is the sweetest, and they're getting married in a few weeks.

I schedule all the social media posts for those pieces, and then a few more links to scientific articles—since science is awesome. Studies on things like the chemistry of love and keeping the spark alive when you've been with someone for a while are vital to the site's reputation as both a fun and intelligent resource for dating tips.

As my half-day nears its end, I check in with Summer, shooting her a text to see how her piece on dates for married couples is going.

Summer: This is a dream come true—plotting dates for my sexy-as-sin husband. I love it.

Teagan: All righty, then. Carry on.

Summer: We will! And I promise the piece will be epic. Want a hint?

Teagan: Do I? Hmm. Wait, of course I do!

Summer: Remember how my misadventures started with The Dating Pool?

Teagan: With your ill-fated letter. Yes, of course.

Summer: Yes. But in retrospect, was it so ill-fated?

Teagan: Considering you're grotesquely, disgustingly, obscenely happy to be married, I'd say no, it wasn't ill-fated at all.

Summer: Exactly! So that's your hint. And I'll be raining down likes, clicks, and shares with my plans.

Teagan: Oh, baby! You're talking my language. See you tomorrow!

I close the text app, say goodbye to Matthew, Rosario, and the rest of the team, then head out of the office to meet up with Bryn at a nearby cruelty-free nail salon that smells like a garden.

It also serves wine—another reason I like Daisy Nails.

Bryn arrives at the same time and gives me a hug.

"Does the boss know you're skipping out early?" she asks me clandestinely, only after whipping her head from side to side to check who might be listening.

"No. Please don't tell Logan when you see him tonight, okay?"

She narrows her eyes, then gives me an *I've got you* nod. "It'll be our secret."

Bryn's boyfriend bought The Dating Pool a year ago

as part of his media firm, and he oversees it as the CEO. Technically, he's my boss, even though I'm not his direct report. But since he signs all our paychecks, he's yet another way we're all tangled up together. We're like a pile of puppies on top of each other, and I don't want to disturb the pack's slumber.

Bryn and I settle into the cushy leather pedicure chairs, dipping our feet into the warm foot tubs and catching up on our week as Daisy brings us glasses of chardonnay.

"Next week, Logan and I leave for our train trip across Canada," Bryn says between sips.

"I want pics and souvenirs. I bet it'll be amazing."

"I can't wait. I do love a road trip of sorts."

"Even better since no one has to drive," I add, then swallow some of the white wine.

"Exactly," she says, and then she shares the latest on some of the new clients at her consulting firm, including her work with the sex-toy company Joy Delivered. That's her flagship client, and I know her work with them well, since Joy Delivered and The Dating Pool share content—we provide dating tips for their site and Joy Delivered offers suggestions on battery-operated friends for the spicy side of our site.

"And how is everything going with the foundation and your fundraising goals?"

"Great," I tell her as the petite blonde who runs the shop asks me to take my right foot out of the water. "Ransom's event was perfect timing. It helped me hit some of my benchmarks for the year, and the board already approved additional funds to give away for the second half of the year, so that makes me very happy."

She lifts her glass to me. "You are both a social media rock star *and* a fundraising rock star. Your parents are insanely proud—you know that, right?"

I love when she refers to them in the present tense. She does that sometimes, and it's because we both try, in our own ways, to keep the memories alive. Bryn's mom was big on sayings and adages, and Bryn often leans on those in trying times. I try to keep the passions of my parents alive by honoring my dad's dying wish—to give so much of what he earned as a billionaire businessman away.

Live well and boldly, but give back too, he told me all throughout his life, but also when he knew he was dying.

I choke up briefly as that time seems to smack me out of nowhere. But then, the memory of his advice doesn't entirely hurt. They are, indeed, words to live by.

"Your mom is proud of you too," I tell my best friend as I lift my glass to hers and clink across the space between us.

She smiles at me, soft and genuine, then a spark of mischief enters her eyes. "Speaking of perfect timing and Ransom . . ."

I shoot her a curious look, daring her to continue. "What about Ransom and me?"

"Well, that's the question, isn't it?"

I roll my eyes because that's easier than digging into the muddy ground of whatever Ransom and I are. Are we anything? Tomorrow might feel like a date to me, but the invitation was to *hang*. I'd do well to remember that. A *hang* is not a date.

"Bryn, we're not dating. We're not together," I say, as much to remind myself as her. I need the reminders more and more these days. I need to stay on the straight and narrow.

"I know, but it feels like you could be . . ." she says, trailing off in a happy tone.

A laugh bursts from my chest. "What does that even mean? *We could be?*"

Setting her glass down, she reaches across the space between our chairs and places her hand on my arm. "I see you guys together. I just do. And I want you to know I'm fine with you going for it. We all are."

Her permission tugs on my heart. Pulls and yanks on that organ in a way I'm not sure I want to be pulled and yanked. "I know that. You've been trying to set me up with him for some time now," I say, trying to make light of her kind words because I'm not entirely sure I'm ready to face what her *blessing* truly means. Especially because I don't know that there's anything to go for. "But we aren't really a thing."

She holds up her hand, moving her fingers together like a mouth. "Blah, blah, blah. Yes, you are.'"

"No, we're not," I fire back.

"*Teagan.*" She says it as cutting as a laser, like she can see through me. And she likely can.

"*Bryn.*"

"I don't want to be the reason you don't explore options with him," she says. "And I think I am. I think we all are. I know your biggest worry is that dating

Ransom might cause our friendship house of cards to crumble."

The gentleness in her voice makes my throat tighten with emotion. But who is it for? I'm not sure, honestly. I've tried to keep emotion at bay for so long. Warding off feelings is safer than having them. When you keep them behind the ramparts, you can't be hurt again and again.

"I can tell you feel something for him," Bryn continues. "If you explore that and it goes badly, or if you explore it and it peters out, we're going to be okay. All of us. Logan and me, Summer and Oliver, Fitz and Dean. We'll be fine, and we'll still be here. For both of you."

Fine.

But would I be fine? And how will I ever know? "It would be awkward. It would be weird," I say, my voice wobbly, as I try to stay the course.

Living behind the walls is easier. The walls are fortified.

Bryn smiles kindly and squeezes my arm. "Life is awkward. Life is weird. We'll manage. I don't want to stand in the way of your happiness with anyone."

I meet her gaze, seeing so much friendship, so much family in her eyes. It knocks loose some of the fear inside me, casts it aside. Maybe frees up some of my worries too. I don't know what Ransom wants, but lately I have a sharper sense of what *I* want. I'm not sure I'm ready to pursue it, but perhaps I will if I can remove this one big obstacle. This fear. The one she's freeing me of. Maybe I shouldn't cling to it any longer. Maybe it's time to let it go. So I ask, "Are you sure?"

She nods decisively. "I'm positive. Don't let us stand in the way. If you want to date him and it doesn't work out, we will be fine. I promise."

I exhale, big and long, picturing possibilities, seeing options. They're fuzzy, hazy, but they're coming into focus. "I don't know what I want," I say, but as those words clip out, they don't feel as true as they did a week ago. "And I don't know what he wants either."

And that . . . that also doesn't seem quite right.

Bryn lifts a brow in curiosity, perhaps hearing the same uncertainty I do—perhaps feeling it too. "Is that true though? That you don't know what you want?"

I absorb her question, turning it over and inside out. As Daisy paints my toes a bright robin's-egg blue, I picture tomorrow, and I start to see how I want it to unfold.

I can see the chance I want to take.

Coming back to the present, I turn to Bryn decisively. "Actually, I do know what I want."

And I proceed to tell her.

13

RANSOM

I am not the fifth wheel.

No way.

I'm so good with this setup. As I fiddle with my tie, waiting for Logan and Oliver along Fifth Avenue, I'm completely cool with heading into Central Park for the wedding with these guys and their women.

Nothing weird about that—about me wandering in with two couples.

Especially since I'm meeting Teagan at the event.

When my friends arrive late Saturday afternoon for the nuptials, dressed in sharp shirts and slacks, Bryn and Summer by their sides, I do not feel like I need to be part of all this two-by-two Noah's Arking. Nope. Not at all.

"Looking good, Ransom," Summer says approvingly as she surveys my attire.

"Same to you—and that ugly git by your side." As I take the teasing jab at Oliver, I think of Teagan and our conversation the other night. I imagine how, if she were here, she'd smile privately at me, knowing my language. Translating smack talk to English the way Tempest translates into ASL.

She'd understand that Oliver's a good bud. Since Fitz hooked me up with this crew, his friends have become my friends too.

Oliver wiggles a brow. "In some areas of England, 'ugly git' is a compliment, so I'll take that, thank you very much."

"Aww, I love you, my ugly git," Summer teases.

"I'm such a lucky ugly git," he says, turning to drop a kiss onto his wife's cheek.

When he does that, my chest has the nerve to pinch.

Whoa.

What's that about?

Oliver can kiss his wife all he wants without me longing for that kind of affection.

I don't need to kiss someone on the cheek or hold hands like any of these lovebirds.

I don't wish for what they have. I swear I don't.

I roll my shoulders, shedding these strange, sudden twinges of . . . *envy.*

There is no room for love-envy in my life.

None whatsoever.

Logan and Bryn stroll over, Logan knocking fists with me then glancing around. "Where's Teagan?"

Yeah, where is she? Why isn't she here yet? Longest wait of my life.

"She'll be here in fifteen minutes," I say quickly.

At the same time, Bryn answers with "She's on her way."

The simultaneous replies do not go unnoticed by Logan, who arches a brow, shooting me a sly look as the five of us wander into the park. "I'd expect Bryn to know what her best friend was up to, but I didn't know you were so intimately acquainted with her schedule too," he says.

As the others walk ahead, I shrug like it's no big deal, cool as a tomcat. "That's when the wedding starts. In fifteen minutes."

He scoffs. "No, dude. In fifteen minutes, it's four forty-five. The wedding starts at five. Being, you know, not dickheads, we all agreed to be here early for our friends getting hitched."

"Exactly. That's why I'm here now." My logic is crumbling, but I'll hold tight to it. Hell, will I ever.

"And you know exactly when Teagan is arriving," he says, like he's busting me.

"Because we're friends." Maybe if I keep up the friend excuse, it will feel more true to me too. I'll convince myself that's the only reason I know when she'll be here. It's definitely not because I've been counting down the seconds until I see her again.

The long, long seconds.

I'm dying to see her.

I can feel it in my chest, this clawing desire to set my eyes on her.

It's intense, and it's terrifying.

Logan sighs, shaking his head, then curls a hand over my shoulder. "Listen, I don't pretend to know everything about women. Or to be an expert on love or second chances."

"But it sounds like you're about to try and fake it," I joke. But this is more deflection than affection. I'm not sure I'm in the mood to turn down the path of Smart Supportive Advice, and it seems he's steering the car thataway.

"Yeah, I am," Logan agrees matter-of-factly. "Because I've learned something in the last two years. Something important. Life comes at you pretty quickly, and a lot of shit happens." He stops in his tracks, letting the others go ahead. "My ex-wife cheated on me."

"I know that, man," I say, sympathy pains spreading in my chest. His story isn't the same as mine, but it's on the same shelf in the bookstore, under the subgenre How to Be Fucked by Love. "I'm sure it must have sucked."

"It did. It was awful, and I felt like shit about myself. Doesn't matter that my ex and I were growing apart. Doesn't matter that I didn't feel a crazy intense connection for her. It hurt, right here," he says, tapping his sternum. "Made me question everything. Made me angry. Made me pissed."

My brow creases, my emotions latching on to those last words as I push back. "I'm not angry."

"I know that, man," he says with a friendly pat on my shoulder. "I do. You're a chill, laid-back dude."

"But . . .?"

What's he getting at?

"But the thing is . . ." He pauses and takes a deep breath, fueling what he's going to say next. "I want you to keep your mind open. I know your ex did a number on you, but that's what exes do simply by being exes. At some point, we have to decide if we want to be defined by the hurts inflicted on us, or to move forward."

I bristle at the notion that I'm holding on to something. And dammit, I realize that bristling proves he's at least somewhere close to the mark. He's poking too close to a sore spot.

"I'm happy, dude," I say. It's a reflex by now, like blocking a move on the ice. "I am."

"But you're happier when you're with Teagan," he says, his eyes zeroed in on me.

He's not wrong, but should we all just do what makes us happy if it's bad for us?

No. That's why you need rules. Why they put a Surgeon General's warning on bottles of whiskey.

"It's too risky," I say emphatically, then gesture to the stone walkway in front of us, the very one that's taking us to our friends' wedding. "Look around. We are all up in each other's business. We hang out—you, me, Fitz, Oliver, Dean now. We're all friends. And the women—they are too. Plus, you own the company where Teagan works. Bryn and Teagan are close friends, and if things ended badly between Teagan and me, your woman would logically side with Teagan and you'd be in a spot."

Logan simply shrugs. "And I'll handle it. But *what if* it leads to happiness for you, man? Is that such a terrible chance to take?"

I heave a sigh, scrubbing a hand across my jaw, trying to get him to feel the weight of the issue, how damn heavy it is. "This isn't just about happiness. It's about being smart. It's about not putting yourself in a position where someone can break you. Not when you know better. Edie was my best friend from college. I crossed the friend-to-girlfriend line once, and look what happened. I was devastated when she ended it. *She* devastated me. I don't want that again, so I've got a rule —don't mess around with a woman who's your friend."

He fixes me with a serious stare. "And by that same logic, I should never get married again, right?"

I blink, parting my lips, stunned speechless by the utter wrongness of that remark. "No," I insist. "You and Bryn are perfect for each other."

"But shouldn't I follow the same rule? Doesn't it apply to me? Don't do the thing that hurt us before, right? You won't get involved with a friend, so maybe I shouldn't ever get married again."

He is goading me, and I hate that I don't have a better reply than "C'mon. That's not what I mean."

"Kind of is though. And if you believe that, now would be a good time to tell me, since I'm asking Bryn to marry me next week."

"Holy shit, man." In spite of the heavy talk, a grin takes over my face, and I yank him in for a quick hug. "That is awesome. I'm so stoked for you."

His smile is magic—he looks like the happiest guy around, and that's saying something, since I'm surrounded by pleased-as-punch fellas. "Thanks. I wish I could speed up time so it was next week now, but I'm also going to enjoy the hell out of every moment with her. Every moment of Fitz and Dean's day today." He takes a beat, drawing a breath. "Do you see what I mean though?"

I look away, at the trees, at the paths winding

through the park, at the crowds starting to gather for Fitz's wedding. At the moments surrounding me. At all my friends, taking chances in their own way. At Fitz, who put his heart on the line for Dean so he could make a life here with the guy he loves. At Oliver, who risked seventeen years of friendship to tell Summer he loved her. And at Logan, a father and a once-married man who was burned, but who's going for a second chance— a second chance at the altar.

Maybe I've had it all wrong.

"I do see what you mean," I say quietly.

Logan slugs my shoulder. "You guys clearly dig each other. And I know you don't want to get on the merry-go-round of love again. I respect that." He meets my gaze, leveling an intensely honest stare at me, something he's been doing a lot of today. "But I wonder if maybe you already have one foot on that carousel?"

My mind slips back to last weekend and how it was with her.

To how I felt with her in the elevator of my building. In my doorway. In my bed.

Well, horny for starters.

But was I happy too?

As I ask myself, I catch a glint of sunlight on red hair, lifting softly in the breeze. Strong legs. A bright, confident smile.

The woman I slept with last week walks toward me.

That's when I fully weigh Logan's questions, and when they don't feel heavy any longer.

Was I happy?

Is that even a question?

I was happy every single second I spent with her.

Every moment—the sex and the talking—was a balm to my soul.

It's making me wonder if it's time to finally reevaluate if the risk is worth it.

My friends are taking all sorts of risks. They're diving headfirst into the waters of love.

Because the reward could be worth it.

Perhaps it's time to let go of my mantra. To let go of my resistance. And to let go of the past.

"Yeah . . . I'm pretty sure I'm already on the carousel and getting dizzy," I admit at last to Logan as Teagan comes closer.

"Then maybe talk to her," he says, then walks away.

He doesn't need to tell me a fifteenth time.

14

RANSOM

I smile as she nears me, and I couldn't stop the grin if I tried. She's gorgeous, but there's so much more to her than looks. I'm keenly aware of the fact that I want to spend the night with her again, but I'm just as eager to spend the next several hours together.

I want Teagan by my side as our friends get married. I want to talk to her, dance with her, toast with her.

"Hey, North," she says when she reaches me.

"Hey, King," I say, as I survey the beauty in front of me, in her green summery dress that shows off the skin of her shoulders—shoulders I want to kiss.

That reveals legs I want to run my hands down.

And that clings to the body I want beside me.

That's only the tip of the iceberg.

There's a helluva lot more to this woman I have a date with in a few days, and I'm going to need to figure out what to do with this growing storm of emotions in my chest. It's not simply desire any longer.

There's more at play. The *more* that drove me to pick

up the phone and talk to her the other night. The *more* that had me asking her to spend some time with me today.

That's why I say, "You look good, *Teagan.*"

Teagan.

Not King.

Time to dispense with the bro-dude talk. Enough of the last names. That's for the guys. I don't want to be one of the guys with her.

"So do you. . . *Ransom*," she says, meeting me on this new terrain, saying my name with a little sweetness, a little suggestiveness.

I step closer and drop a kiss onto her cheek, brushing my lips across her skin.

A gust of breath escapes her lips, then a soft, lingering *ohhh.*

"Hey," I say when I step back, woozy from the strawberry scent of her. "It's good to see you."

"Likewise." She sounds the slightest bit shy, then she shucks that off as she says, "I was looking forward to this all day."

"To the wedding?" Because she can't mean anything else. Can she?

"Yes, to the wedding. I love weddings. But also," she says, taking a beat, her eyes flashing with a hint of nerves that she blinks away, "to seeing you."

My heart hammers at words I didn't let myself hope for. My skin warms at her admission.

This woman makes me feel so damn good—in my body and right in my heart.

Those words she said should scare me.

They ought to terrify me.

But when I'm with Teagan, I'm everything Logan said I was, everything I haven't truly been since Edie—*I'm happy.*

I drag a hand through my hair. It's decision time.

Do I still want to toe all my lines?

Heed all my mantras?

Or will I kick them to the side?

I swallow past the roughness in my throat and take a step closer to what I want. "Want to go on a date with me? To see our guys get hitched?"

Her smile lights the sky. "You bet I do," she says, and we walk the rest of the way together.

I return to what she said a few seconds ago as we stroll past a tree with white blossoms. "Tell me why you love weddings."

Her response is breezy. "Why does anyone love weddings?"

I shoot her a *give me more* look. "I don't know why anyone else loves them. But I want to know why *you* do," I say, and I'm driven by the need to know her more, to understand her. "That's why I asked."

I expect her to say the dress, or the vows, or the way they make her feel.

She turns her face to me, taking a beat, the cogs in her brain whirring, I can tell. "I love rituals. I kind of can't get enough of them."

"Why is that?" I'm intrigued by her answer. Once upon a time, she was simply a funny girl, and I liked that about her. She was free and easy, a hoot to play games with. In this last week, she's peeled back new layers, shown me other sides, and those sides draw me in just as much as her humor does.

"I think we need them desperately as a society. The before, the after, the way rituals mark a new phase in our lives. Weddings, of course, do that. They're not only a declaration in words but in deeds too. You're leaving one stage behind and stepping into a new future. I think celebrations to mark those changes are so necessary for our hearts"—she slides a hand briefly over her chest then taps her temple—"and our heads."

I noodle on that as we near the other guests, letting her observations sink in. "I expected you to say something else. But that makes beautiful sense. I get it. I get it completely."

She meets my gaze, her blue eyes etched with intensity. "Right? I think we need the acknowledgment to see us through both good times and bad."

"To guide us through the insanity around us." I wave toward the city behind me to indicate the topsy-turvy madness of the world today.

"Yes. Life is *only* uncertain. Life is *only* unpredictable."

Hell, she's the expert. She knows this better than any of us, losing her family the way she did.

She goes on as we reach the friends and relatives here for Fitz and Dean. "Birthdays, celebrations, weddings, graduations, funerals. All of it helps us to process the unpredictable unknowns around us."

Unknowns.

That's exactly what Logan was getting at earlier. I think about my own fears—the great, big unknown that is everything that might happen if I step over the line with Teagan.

What it would do to our friendship.

What it would do to our friends.

What it would do to me.

I don't have those answers. No one does—until they invent time travel, I suppose. But maybe I'm ready to face that uncertainty because the woman I want to spend the next several hours with—and a whole lot longer—is so damn brave.

Braver than I am.

Knowing that, feeling that, makes my heart beat a little faster for her.

This is the moment. I take a step closer, reach for her hand, and hold it as the grooms walk to the justice of the peace.

She squeezes my fingers back, and like that, we watch our friends get married.

As they say their vows, I understand why Teagan loves rituals. There's something intensely powerful about witnessing this moment.

Plus, it's pretty fucking cool to see one of the toughest defensemen in the NHL, a guy who has my back on the ice in every damn game, pledging to be with one person for the rest of his life.

It's a before and an after.

And most of all, it's a choice.

When they say I do, a kernel of something bitter that had staked a claim inside me since Edie left cracks further, halves down the middle, and maybe, finally, it crumbles to nothing.

Or perhaps it's that I've finally decided it's time to let go of that line I was holding.

To say goodbye to the past and not look back.

Maybe that's my private ritual. One I didn't even know I needed until I watched this public one.

This vibrant and powerful celebration of love.

15

RANSOM

Normally, when it comes to weddings, I'm a take-it-or-leave-it kind of person.

Weddings are . . . fine.

They're full of people milling about, talking, eating.

They're perfectly acceptable.

Not my first choice for a weekend activity. Not when there are things like pickup basketball, comedy clubs, concerts, barbecues, soccer, and any other type of reasonably organized sports as options.

But this wedding is cool as hell.

It's relaxed. It's easy. It's just two people getting hitched, having a meal, and sharing it with their friends.

I indulge in some fantastic appetizers, like stuffed mushrooms and sushi rolls, along with a couple of glasses of champagne. Most of the time, I'm a beer guy, but when there's champagne, I can't resist.

And this shit is just so damn good.

I raise my third glass of bubbly to Teagan as we lean against the bar. Before I can offer up a third toast—our prior toasts were to playlists from teen-centric TV shows (her idea) and to comedy albums from sarcastic, offbeat comedians (my idea)—a booming voice lands on my ears.

"Ah, don't let me interrupt another delicious *momento romántico*."

It's Martinez. Of course—he's buds with Fitz.

I roll my eyes. "But you're so good at it, Marty Boy."

He parks an elbow on the bar and looks at Teagan. "You weren't really going to kiss a man who doesn't have a ring, were you?" He waggles his fingers, displaying his championship ring from when the Yankees won the World Series a couple of years ago.

Damn good series.

And I burn with jealousy, since I don't have a championship yet.

So I need another way in. "I get it. All those endless innings twiddling your thumbs on the bench have you confused. But let me clarify. We have cups—they're bigger and better."

"Ah, thank you," he says, with a faux appreciative nod. Then, in an innocent tone, he asks, "And where's yours?"

Teagan turns to me, hands on her hips, sass in her eyes. "Yeah, where is your Stanley Cup, North? Because this time next year, I want to be drinking champagne from it."

I laugh and haul her in close. "Me too, King. Me too," I say, and at this moment, we are friends. But we're something more too, and it feels good to laugh like this, all of us together. I like it a lot.

"By the way, thank you for that cut fastball last night," Teagan says to the closer, "striking out the side with the bases loaded. I hate Boston with a deep passion."

Martinez brings his hand to his heart. "That is the most beautiful thing anyone has ever said. I, too, despise them to the depths of my soul. Beating them is my joy, as I was telling—" He cuts himself off, shifting gears suddenly. "Did you enjoy the wedding, Teagan?"

"It was wonderful—every second. And who were you telling about your disdain for the Red Sox?" she asks, something about where he stopped catching her curiosity.

With a light laugh, Martinez waves a hand, dismissing the question. "Just someone I was chatting with this morning."

Her eyes light up. "Was it your mystery bidder? Did you ever find out who your phone bidder was?"

A hint of a smile flashes across his features, but he quickly erases it. "I'll find out tomorrow. Until then, I need to go mingle. Have fun, *tortolitos*." He winks, then adds a translation, "Lovebirds, that is."

Teagan's cheeks flush pink. It's a good look on her.

Martinez leaves, heading to join the other guests, going to talk to Fitz's sister. "Maybe one of Fitz's sisters was the mystery bidder," I suggest.

"He only has one single sister—Emma, the one who studies art."

"Oh yeah. She's a hoot. We used to mess with Fitz and pretend we were going to be a thing."

Teagan's eyes turn fiery. She breathes through her nostrils.

I try to rein in a grin. "Are you jealous?"

"A little."

I laugh. "Holy fuck, that's adorable. Jealousy looks good on you, Teagan." She folds her arms, and I bump my shoulder against hers. "As I said, it looks good on you."

She rolls her eyes, then picks up her glass, lifting it. "To friendships and good-looking jealousies, then."

"To friendship, rituals, and wild unknowns."

I clink my glass to hers, take another sip, then set the flute on the bar, gazing briefly at the New York City skyline visible through the windows of the Loeb Boathouse. Not a bad way to spend a night.

This isn't the first wedding I've been to in the last two years. I attended Summer and Oliver's a few months ago. But this is the first one where I'm not mulling over what-might-have-beens.

I'm *only* thinking about my life right now. About what might happen tonight. And tomorrow. And the next day.

I feel unburdened for the first time in a long while, and it's a great feeling.

Teagan takes a sip, then puts her glass down next to mine. "So, how would you rate this wedding?"

I rub my palms together, ready to dive into the review. "Bring it on. What's the scale? I need to know exactly how I'm grading it."

She gazes at the ceiling, as if deep in thought. "On a scale of one to . . . better than a chocolate milkshake."

I pretend to stumble backward. "Whoa. Those are fighting words, Teagan."

She maintains a straight face. "I know. I'm asking you to make a very tough choice."

I draw a deep breath, like I'm seriously considering this. And I am. I do love chocolate milkshakes fiercely, and that gives me an idea. "There's only one way to find out."

She arches a curious brow. "How good this wedding is?"

"Yes," I say emphatically.

"Okay, enlighten me. How do we find out how good this wedding is?"

I roll my eyes like it's so damn obvious. "We should get a milkshake after this."

"Nope. My question. My rules. You have to judge before you get dessert."

"Woman, you are a fierce competitor."

She wiggles her brows. "I know. Now answer the question."

Before I can, Fitz wanders back in from the deck of the boathouse, Dean by his side. My teammate catches my eye, a knowing glint in his eyes as he glances from me to Teagan and mouths, *Go for it.*

I mouth back, *I can't hear you,* just to fuck with him.

I turn back to the redhead who is under my skin and in my head. She's tapping her toe, pursing her lips. "I know you guys were just exchanging words about me," she says, but she's laughing, and I love that about her.

She gets me.

She understands how I am with my friends. She

doesn't judge me for how I like to have fun with the guys.

She doesn't want to change me.

She's cool with who I am.

Yes, the bitter kernel I've nurtured, I've watered, I've held on to—it's all gone. And I'm so damn glad.

I lift my hand, set it on her shoulder, then slide it down her arm. "Actually, here's my answer to the is-it-better-than-a-milkshake question. There's only one thing that'll make this wedding better than a chocolate milkshake," I say, my voice a little low, a little rough, emotions seeping into it that I didn't entirely expect.

But ones I don't want to stop.

She shivers, her gaze drifting to my hand on her arm. Her eyes swing back up to mine. "And what's that?"

I lean in close and whisper in her ear, "If you'll dance with me."

Perhaps this was always inevitable tonight.

It feels like it can't be any other way as she brushes her lips against my neck, up to my ear, softly, sweetly, saying, "Yes. That would make it the best."

"Pillowtalk" plays by Zayn, and I'm not a fifth wheel.

I don't give a fuck what anyone else is doing as I take Teagan's hand and guide her to the dance floor.

Her body glides against mine. We fit together like we don't have to think about where hands go, where arms go.

Because everything feels natural with her. Everything feels real and true.

My arms loop around her waist. Hers rope around

my neck. The lights twinkle, the music pulses, and our bodies sway.

We're on the edge of the hardwood floor, moving in a slow, intoxicating rhythm. My hand travels up the small of her back. Somehow she snuggles closer. "That feels nice," she murmurs.

"Nice? Just nice?" I tease.

"Nice isn't good enough for you?" she taunts in a flirty whisper.

"Nice isn't how I'm feeling right now," I say as I bend my face into the crook of her neck, whispering those words in her ear.

"Mmm." She tugs me closer, her hands tightening around my neck. "How are you feeling, Ransom?"

I press against her, the evidence hard and clear as my pelvis aligns with her body. "How do you think I feel?"

Her breath hitches. "I could guess, but maybe spell it out."

I laugh lightly, pull back to meet her gaze, then break our hold for a few seconds to spell it out with my hands.

"What did you say?" she asks, as I circle my hands back around her.

"Something dirty," I murmur.

"I figured out that much," she says, her fingers tangling in the back of my hair in a way that drives me crazy.

"I love that," I whisper.

"When I touch your hair?"

I nod against her. "Yeah, it turns me all the way on."

"That is very good to know, since I kind of love having my hands in your hair. It's so soft and lush, and it gets me excited," she says as she runs her hands through my hair again.

My breath catches from her soft, nimble touch. "Now I'm getting more aroused," I say roughly.

"I can tell, and I like it."

"I think it's chocolate milkshake time."

Her lips dust across my neck, journeying to my jaw. She leaves kisses there, and it feels like she's marking me with gentle but still possessive kisses. "Are you sure you want to get a milkshake?"

I slide my lips along her neck, traveling to her ear. "I feel like we could skip it. You?"

She nods quickly, purposefully. "Yes."

We barely bother to say goodbye to our friends.

I'm confident they won't care.

Actually, that's not true.

I'm confident this is what they want.

And it's what I want now too.

Without reservations, without rules.

16

TEAGAN

I take one last look behind me—a parting glance at the beautiful tableau.

This is what I never want to lose.

The friendships. The moments. The way these people have all become my family.

My *found* family. The one I desperately needed.

But seeing all of them, tangled up in each other, makes everything so clear.

There are no guarantees for any of us.

We walk down aisles.

We pledge to love each other.

We promise forever.

We hope we get all the years.

I'm not ready for those kinds of promises, but I'm ready to live again.

To feel again.

To knock down my walls and let the light in.

I don't want to lose what's in front of me, but as I

take a mental snapshot, I'm keenly aware that all these men and women took a risk to be where they are.

Summer and Oliver risked friendship.

After brutal divorces, Bryn and Logan chose honesty and trust for a second chance.

Dean moved across an ocean for Fitz, who made it possible for them both.

None of those happily ever afters were especially easy. But all are worth it.

I don't know what's inside my story. But I'd like to keep turning the pages.

Yes, I've been burned, I've been hurt, and I've lost.

But in these months of being Ransom's friend, I've tasted the potential of new chances.

The possibilities that come with risk.

The pluses of being more than the woman who likes to have a good time, more than the sassy chick marching to the beat of her single-in-the-city soundtrack.

Because last week I told myself the greatest lie of all —that I would get him out of my system in only one night. A few days later, I learned that I don't want him anywhere but *in.*

This man is in my system, and I want him there, no matter the risks.

With one last lingering look at all the happy people, I turn around and step toward the risk I'm choosing to take.

* * *

I hold open the door to my apartment, then let it close softly behind me, kicking off my shoes.

Ransom toes off his and steps back, looking around. "Cool digs, but can I please have the nickel tour later?"

"Who said I was even giving you a tour at all?"

He laughs, then follows me up the first flight of stairs, and when we reach the landing, his jaw drops. "Is this the second floor? You have two floors?"

I hold up three fingers, smiling as we turn into the living room.

"Hot damn. I would make an ice rink out of one of the floors."

I laugh. "Yes, admittedly, that was next in my plans."

"Good plan. I'll get my skates."

"I'll get the Zamboni."

"A woman after my own heart." He wraps his arms around my waist and hoists me over his shoulder. "And now I will take the tour of your bed, please."

I pound my fists playfully on his back, taunting, "See if you can find my bedroom."

"It can't be that hard," he teases, carrying me to the hallway, then stopping in his tracks.

"Holy shit, you have a big hallway too," he says, setting me down.

"Hey, I thought you were carrying me." I pout.

"I was, then I saw more of your place."

"Gawker," I tease as his eyes swing up and down the long hallway that leads to three bedrooms.

He gestures wildly down the hall. "What do you do with all this space?"

I shrug. "Not much. I don't go into all the empty

rooms. I should sell it, I guess, but I also like it. It's where I grew up."

"I like it too," he says, then waves a hand like he's dismissing it. "But you know what?"

"What?"

He wiggles his brows. "Let's go to your room."

I bump my hip against his. "Hello? I was trying to take you there."

"Take me there now, woman."

I lead him to my bedroom, open the door, and bring him to my bed. We strip out of our clothes, and when I run my hands along his carved chest, I let out a long, happy sigh.

This feels right.

This feels like where I want to be—taking this chance, wherever it leads.

17

RANSOM

What a difference a week makes.

Sure, the vibe between us changed the night of the auction. Everything felt different as soon as the evening began, as we walked to the event.

But now, as I sit on the edge of her bed, pull her on top of me, and thread my fingers through her hair, *we* feel different.

In all the right ways.

And I need to let her know.

I need to tell her before we move on to the main attraction. "Teagan," I say, steeling myself to say the hard stuff—hard for me, that is.

"Yes?" Her voice is shuddery.

"Let's make a deal," I say, using the same words we used last time we were together. Except not . . .

She tenses in my arms. "What sort of deal?"

I swallow roughly, pushing past my fears. "Let's make a deal to let this be what it's going to be."

"The sex?" Her voice pitches up.

I shake my head adamantly. "No. The *us.*"

Us. I've avoided being an *us* for years. But I don't want to stop coming together with her.

Teagan's lips curve into a grin, slow and warm. "You and me?"

I nod, bringing her close, dusting a kiss across her jaw. "I don't think it's going to be *just* one night."

"And you don't want to stay *just* friends?"

"I *want* to be friends. But I also want to be more with you." It's a terrifying statement to say out loud, but a wonderful one to give voice to as well. "I want to see you. I want to date you. I want to spend time in and out of bed, just you and me."

"I want that so much too." She sounds woozy, delighted.

I grin wildly as I thread my fingers through her soft red strands. "Let's see what this is between us. Let's find out what the hell we're all about. No rules, no limits. Just us."

"Count on it," she says, then she grabs my face and crushes her lips to mine. Her kiss is fierce and hot. She's full of passion and need, and she kisses me without inhibitions, without fear.

I kiss her back the same way, pouring all the possibilities of *us* into the way we connect.

The kiss spreads through my whole body, radiating in my bones. It's intense and deep, and it feels like a whole new brand of kissing.

It's more than just the heat and need of last week.

It's something else entirely.

It's intimate and free. We are two people who don't want to be hurt, but who are willing to jump anyway.

And the kiss also makes me horny as hell.

Because, well, the woman of my dreams is naked and wet and grinding against me.

Our connection rockets higher, burning brighter as I adjust Teagan on my lap, sliding my fingers between her legs, gliding them through all that fantastic, delicious wetness.

I break the kiss, groaning. "You're so fucking wet," I say, savoring the slippery feel of her.

She reaches for my cock, stroking it. "And you're so fucking hard."

"Seems we should do something about both these problems right now," I say, and she grabs a condom from the nightstand, slides it on me, and then rises up, rubbing my dick against her center.

She moans, a delicious, erotic sound that carries across the room as she strokes my cock against her sweet, lovely pussy.

She drops her head back, letting her hair spill behind her as she lowers onto my length.

"Fuuuuuck," I groan as she sinks down, taking me all the way inside her.

Exactly where I want to be.

Her lips fall open, parting on a gorgeous O as she slams her hands down on my shoulders, curling them over me, clutching tightly. "I want to just sit on your cock all night."

I laugh lightly, then give the only right answer. "Please do."

"Dear God, you feel incredible," she says, barely moving, just adjusting, rocking, *taking*.

Then, after a few deliriously sexy seconds, she swivels her hips.

It's mind-bending, watching her seek her pleasure. My skin sizzles. I'm burning up from the vision of Teagan taking me deep, finding her own pace.

"Ride me, sunshine. Just fucking ride me till you come so damn hard," I tell her as I grip her hips, my fingers digging into her flesh as she grinds down, then rises up.

She moans and groans, her hands tightening around my neck, her tits bouncing so beautifully against my chest.

Her eyes fall shut as she uses my dick for her pleasure.

My dick likes to be used for that so very much.

"That's right. Use me to get yourself off, sunshine," I say, urging her on as she rides me hard and deep.

She's fierce and wild in bed, seeking what she wants, owning her desire, and it's the sexiest thing I've ever seen. It turns me on everywhere in my body, my cells sparking, my bones vibrating as I watch her chase her bliss.

Her noises grow louder, more erratic. Her breath comes faster, harder.

Then her nails dig into my shoulder, and she freezes, then keens, shouting *"Oh God"* over and over as she shudders, coming on my cock.

And her orgasm unlocks my own as I climax so damn hard, I swear I see stars.

And maybe I see a future with this woman too.

That's something I didn't think I'd want ever again, but I'm sure I want it desperately now.

18

RANSOM

I didn't think I was a gawker, but maybe I am. Because, holy shit . . . this house is insane.

I could get lost in here. There are probably trapdoors and secret attics. Underground bunkers maybe.

The next morning after I put on my boxer briefs and hit the little boys' room, I wander down the hall, amazed at the size of everything. I think the hallways are sprouting hallways and the stairs are giving birth to more steps.

Not wanting to spy, I return to her bedroom, standing in the doorway. Teagan's still sound asleep, flat on her stomach, splayed out like a starfish, her red hair a fan around her head.

Snuggling would be nice, but I'm pretty wired, so I quietly snag my phone from the nightstand and head to the living room.

As I survey the spacious digs, I consider whether to sit on the couch or the chaise longue. Or the other couch.

Or the window seat.

I shake my head in disbelief. She has a fucking window seat.

Well, there is no contest.

I am sitting in the window seat. Bring me a cup of tea and a well-worn book, and I might as well just spend a rainy day here. If I were good at selfies, I'd snap a shot of myself and title it *"Reading Nook."*

But it's June, and the sun is already rising in a blue sky that promises a perfect New York day.

I settle in against the green, purple, and blue pillows spilling across the window seat and click open my phone.

My screen is bursting with notifications.

Text after text.

Logan: And good night to you too.

Logan: I mean, not that I need a goodbye, but holy hell. That was one hell of an exit. You took off like a fighter jet.

Smiling, I tap out a reply.

Ransom: Why, thank you. I consider that the highest of compliments.

But that's not quite enough for the man who set me straight last night. Every now and then, a guy needs to speak a different language with his buds. I send another text.

Ransom: And I hope you know that this is the highest of compliments—thank you for the bro talk last night. I needed it, and I appreciate it.

Logan: Well, then, I couldn't be happier.

Ransom: Bet you'll be happier after you ask Bryn to marry you. Let me know when she says yes.

Logan: Aww, you're sweet. Did it pain you to be honest like that?

Ransom: Like ripping off a limb, but every now and then, I gotta be up-front.

Logan: Wish me luck. Also, good luck to you, man.

Next, there's a message from Fitz. I furrow my brow, wondering what the hell he's doing texting me when he's taking off for his honeymoon.

Fitz: Say it. I was right. I was motherfucking right.

Fitz: I'm waiting to use my *I told you so* and receive my thank you, all rolled into one big mea culpa from you, dickhead.

Fitz: I told you she'd be good for you, and I told you to go for it.

Fitz: And I was right. Also, did you or did you not score on my wedding night? I'm like a good luck charm.

The flurry of messages was sent an hour ago. It's nine thirty, so I reply.

Ransom: What the fuck are you texting me for? Don't you have more important things to do . . . like, say, fly to Copenhagen for your honeymoon?

Fitz: I was in line grabbing coffee at the airport, asshole. SINCE I WAS UP ALL NIGHT. Also, I can almost always make time to give you shit. Now, we're about to take off, and inquiring minds want to know. WHEN DO I GET MY THANK YOU?

Ransom: Thanks for last night, you jackass. There, happy?

Fitz: Yes! I knew it. I was right. I was motherfucking right. You and Teagan are a thing. Called it.

Ransom: Go to Denmark, cupid. Just go to Denmark and have fun with your hubby.

Fitz: Obviously.

One more note from him lands on my phone.

Fitz: Also, I might have been part of that bet with Martinez and Carnale at the auction.

My brow creases as I think back to the night of the auction.

Ransom: Which one? There were about a gazillion.

Fitz: The one for a grand on whether she'd kiss you if she won you. Carnale said she wouldn't. Martinez said she would. But guess what? I put my neck on the line. I said YOU'D kiss her. I had to defend your honor, bro.

I laugh, recalling the kiss. Yeah. I went first.

Ransom: I kissed her. You defended well. Happens every now and then.

Fitz: Sort of like your sense of humor. Also, see you on the flip side. I'm off.

Ransom: Hey! One more thing. Congrats! I'm really fucking happy for you.

Fitz: Thanks, man. Means a lot to me. And now I really am outta here.

Then, finally, a note from Martinez blinks at me.

Martinez: So, about that bet . . .

Ransom: Which one? Be specific. There's the one where I beat you in the auction—aka the one where you pony up all your teeny little greenbacks for my favorite charity. Then there's the one where you and your catcher bet each other that my woman wouldn't kiss me.

Martinez: Oh, she is your woman now? *Felicidades.*

I'm about to write back and ask again which bet he was referring to when the padding of soft feet lands on my ears. I set the phone down, cross the living room, and grin when I see Teagan yawning, stretching her hands above her head, then smiling at me. She's wearing sleep shorts and a tank top, and I want to kiss her everywhere.

"I see you found my reading nook," she says.

My heart thumps hard. So hard it might be trying to leap out of my chest.

"And I think I'd like to take a pic and post it on the Instagram feed for hot guys in reading nooks," she adds.

"Is that a thing?" I ask as I close the remaining few feet between us.

"If not, I'm starting that hashtag today."

"Give me a paperback, and I'll pose for you."

"Ooh, you know how to tempt me," she murmurs, then she sighs as I band an arm around her back, thread a hand through her hair, and claim her lips in a sweet, minty morning kiss. Briefly, she breaks the kiss, whispering, "Brushed my teeth for you. No morning breath here."

"Dude. Same for you," I say, smiling against her mouth then kissing her again.

Deeper this time.

My head swims with desire—and something else too.

Something stronger, more powerful.

Something that tethers me to her, and I know what it is as my lips sweep across hers.

It's everything I've avoided for the last two years.

It's everything I've tried to protect myself from.

The feeling that she's the only one I want. That we could be together. That we could be a thing.

As I kiss her more deeply, our tongues skating over each other, our mouths searching, I wish for more weekends like this, more times with her, and, most of all, I hope she feels the same way.

When I break the kiss, she blinks several times. "Good morning to me," she says.

I smile, and it feels like nothing can make me stop. "Hey, I wanted to revise something about our deal."

"The no-rules deal?" She slides her hands up my pecs then down my abs.

"Yes. That one."

"Okay," she says tentatively, then squares her shoulders, taking a deep breath. "Lay it on me."

She's so tough, so strong. I can see that tenacity in her blue eyes, in the way she stands. She's bracing herself for something hard, for something unexpected.

Maybe from years of doing precisely that.

But I hope that what I have to say is something she'll want to hear.

I press a kiss to her forehead. "When I said no rules, I was foolish. I have a very big rule." I pull back, meeting her gaze. "Just you and me. That's the one rule. I don't want to find some guy's vanilla-honey lotion in your bathroom, okay?"

She laughs, her nose crinkling. "Or his lavender deodorant?"

I nod, big and long, teasing her. "And no hairbrushes, K? Keep those all away. You hear me now?"

She raises her hand, ruffling my hair. "Do you need a hairbrush though?"

"I thought you liked my messy hair," I say, dropping a kiss onto her cheek, loving the freedom to embrace her like this. I flash back to laser tag the other week, to all the little touches we exchanged. They were all precursors, it seems, to what we both really wanted.

"I love your messy hair," she says, then slides her fingers through it. "And yes, Ransom North. I want you all to myself. I like you a lot. In fact," she says, licking her lips, taking a deep breath, "I'm kind of crazy for you."

My heart spins wildly, the merry-go-round picking up speed and turning in whip-fast circles. "What do you know? I'm kind of crazy about you too."

I haul her close for another hot, deep kiss that makes my head hazy and my skin tingle. And, big shock, it makes me want more than kissing. She seems to feel that way too, judging from how she's melting against me, wriggling against me. And, oh yeah, grinding too.

Good morning indeed.

We stumble over to the nearest couch, stripping off the little we have on. We tangle together, kissing more, touching everywhere. I slide my hand between her legs, my skin sizzling as I glide across her hot, wet center.

"Need a condom," I mutter.

She props her cheek in her hand, nibbling on the

corner of her lip. "Or . . . we could go without. I'm clean and on protection."

I groan, slide a hand up her neck, and grip her hair. "Me too. Clean, that is."

I flip her to her back, hike her legs around my waist, and slide home. Pleasure envelopes me everywhere, from my toes to my hair.

She arches against me, her lips falling open, a shudder moving through her.

I thrust into her, fucking her on the couch. She moans and cries out, moving with me, rocking against me, gripping my hair, yanking me close.

She wraps her legs nice and tight around me, tugging me nearer as her fingers rope through my hair.

It's hot and frenzied and passionate.

And somehow it feels both like fucking and like a promise.

Like we're sealing our deal.

To be with each other.

To move past all our fears and jump into the great, wide waters of trying again.

With someone you trust.

Someone you're pretty damn sure you could love.

That's how sex with her feels.

Soon, we're both panting, moaning, and coming together, tangled, sweaty, and satisfied.

* * *

A little later, after we shower, she gives me the tour, showing me the three-story brownstone she grew up in and all the pictures of her family, telling me stories as we go.

Every second feels precious and important.

When we're done, I turn to her in the kitchen, linking her fingers with mine. "I love knowing all that. Thank you for sharing."

"It's always been easy to talk to you," she says. "We're just expanding our repertoire."

I tilt my face. "You know, that's a good way to put it. Speaking of, I'm supposed to see Luna and Tempest today. Do you want to meet my sisters?"

"I'd love to."

Maybe we're zooming through these moments quickly.

But maybe not.

Because everything feels right about this pace, and this woman, and this new future we're stepping into.

The only thing that throws me is when we meet up again in an hour. My phone is buzzing, and it's Tempest saying she has something to tell me.

19

RANSOM

Teagan gives me a tentative look when we reach the coffee shop. "I can just wait outside, or run errands and meet you back here," she offers.

I shake my head, having none of that. "She knows I'm with you. It's fine."

Teagan chuckles, patting my shoulder in a *you're so cute* fashion. "That isn't the issue. I meant if you wanted to see her alone."

"No, we can go together. It's all crazy talk anyway."

I show her the text again.

Tempest: It's about Adrian.

"I mean, she has to be playing a joke on me," I say, then push open the door to the coffee shop, scanning the tables for my sister. She's in the back, tapping away on her computer.

I march over to her, introduce her to Teagan, then grab a chair and park myself in it.

"So . . . is this the height of smack talk?"

She grins. "I assure you it's not. It's all true. I'm seeing Adrian Martinez."

My. Jaw. Drops.

Clangs to the floor.

I grab it, yank it back up.

"Seriously?"

Tempest grins wickedly. "Yes, seriously."

Teagan holds up a palm to high-five. "You go, girl."

I snap my gaze to my woman. "How can you be encouraging her?"

Teagan rolls her pretty eyes. "Adrian's a fascinating guy, and you're friends. What is the problem?"

I huff. She makes a good point. But the problem is . . . "How did this happen?"

Teagan laughs again and sets a hand on my arm. "Sweetie, you can't figure it out?"

"No. And why are you looking at me like I'm clueless?"

Teagan meets Tempest's gaze. "You're his phone bidder, right?"

Tempest smiles proudly. "I am indeed. We had lunch this week, and have met up a few more times already."

Teagan's eyes light up. "We should all go out together."

"I'd love that," Tempest says, then looks at me. "And you would too, right, Ransom?"

She's leading the witness. She's saying what she wants me to say.

And part of me wants to growl and grump, but another part realizes my sister is happy, my woman is happy, and hell, maybe my bud is too.

"Sure. Let's double."

It sounds odd, but oddly cool too.

20

TEAGAN

Two weeks later

I strut down the street on the way to work, pop music blasting, my sassy pink purse on my arm, bopping in my head to the beat of my . . . no-longer-single-in-the-city lifestyle.

I've been with Ransom—officially—for only two weeks.

But it's been a whirlwind.

A fantastic fourteen days of dates and sex, nights and talks, food and fun. And more sex.

As well as falling for him.

Falling so much it ought to scare me.

But I'm not scared.

Or at least I'm not scared enough to stop it.

I'm brave enough to try it.

And when I arrive at work and open my email, I'm reminded why.

Summer sent in her dating article, and when I open the file, I can't stop smiling.

She and Oliver wrote love letters to each other about their married dates, and it reminds me that this is why love is worth taking a chance on. Because sometimes friendships don't just become something more— they become everything.

I sink back in my chair with the letters and devour them.

* * *

Dear Sexy-As-Sin Husband,

Let's talk about dating your husband.

Well, *my* husband.

You, obviously, and the date starts here in this letter.

First, have I told you lately how good you look in your Speedo?

Or how freaking adorable you are when you get out of bed with your hair sticking up in ten thousand directions?

Or how cute you are even if you have a cookie crumb on the corner of your lips?

Well, I don't always tell you that *last* one. Sometimes I

just lick it off. Because cookies and your lips are the perfect combo.

Point being—I dig you.

In the water, out of the water, at home, in the park, in the morning, and at night.

And sometimes you need to let your LOL know. (That's Love of Your Life. Which, fine, would technically be LOYL, but LOL is funnier.)

So, allow me to romance you, epistolary-style. Because romance is a key part of dating my husband—something I always want to do.

It's never a challenge, because you will always be the man I love, and you will always be my sexy-as-sin favorite—and now one and only—ex-boyfriend.

And, lucky me, as your wife and roomie, I get to luxuriate in the proof of that whenever I wish. All I have to do is pull back the sheets one lazy Sunday morning. Or linger at the end of swim class and wait for you to emerge from the pool—those arms, that chest, and that . . . ahem.

Yes, I linger. Yes, I check you out.

Can you blame me?

My hubs is a solid one hundred on the one-to-ten babe-o-meter.

Every now and then, though, I feel like I don't see your face as much as I want.

Fine, we did have fun power-eating Life cereal together the other morning before you rushed to take a client call and I had to jet to go for a run with Mags. And yes, admittedly, we played footsie under the table the other night at Gin Joint with our friends.

Those things are great.

But I don't want to lose the magic that brought us together.

Between your successful firm and my new gym finding its feet, it can be difficult to sneak away for those little moments together. The things that make us unique. The things that make us *us*.

Dating.

We were masterful daters before we were engaged.

And I want to keep coming up with fantastic ways to date.

Like we did the other night—so simple, so in character for us.

You surprised me by picking me up from the pole-dancing class Roxanne insisted I try, and you took me to that new diner just a hop, kiss, and jump away from Central Park.

And *ohmyword*. If grilled cheese could become president, I would vote, vote, vote for that sexy contender.

It had the perfect level of melt and the right amount of pickle, and it left my taste buds in some kind of comfort food heaven.

But that wasn't my favorite part of the evening.

After the diner, which we unanimously agreed made a good second- choice last meal—because nothing could top Melt My Heart—we indulged in a bit of PDA (I can't resist kissing you!) while we sipped cocktails at Gin Joint and planned our next vacation. The pictures you painted of gorgeous summer days under the Eiffel Tower, of quaint French bistros with intimate lighting and tables set for two, and of hot summer nights spent twisted between the sheets . . . you had me at *bonjour*.

And let me just say—*Ooh la la, voulez vous coucher avec moi ce soir?*

Vacation-browsing is the new thrift-shopping. It's a perfect date-night activity because I want to go everywhere with my favorite person.

But that wasn't the best part of the evening either.

Later, as we walked home, a delish blend of liquor and lust and love fueled my steps. We stopped at the door to our building. You pulled me close, and with the crazy, wild symphony of New York in the background—the cars, the lovers, the sirens, the laughter—you kissed me. That kiss was loaded with the promise of more and the certainty of forever, and *that right there*.

And *that* was the absolute highlight of the date with my husband.

Well, that, and what happened next when we went up to our apartment. But that's a tale for our eyes only.

I loved our latest date, and it reminded me that we will always be us. With our busy lives, all we need is the simplest of things—like a pole, some grilled cheese, and our favorite watering hole—and we reconnect.

In the meantime, I will leave you with this—what walks like a duck and has feathers like a duck, but talks like something else entirely?

You'll find out tomorrow when I pick you up after work for our next date.

With all my love,

Your Wife

* * *

Dear Hilarious, Sexy, Brilliant, Fantastic Wife of Mine,

Yes, let's talk about dating.

You, my cupcake, are a pro.

You are a masterful dater.

But this should come as no surprise. Haven't you been cooking up brilliant schemes for years?

You have, and let's be honest—this bloody fantastic union we've got going on is your greatest scheme yet.

And I'm so damn grateful you're *my* brilliant schemer.

I have all the evidence one could want attesting to your date-planning skills.

You made me *like* a candle-making class.

That should have been impossible.

But you took me to one, and that night you introduced me to all the delights of candle wax.

Brilliant and beautiful—that's the woman I married.

Do you know what else I've learned since I've dated you?

I've learned to never say never.

Never close the door on a crazy class, because the next fantastic night could be right around the corner.

Though, admittedly, I never thought our next date would be an art class.

You already know how I feel about classes, cupcake.

And a how-to-paint-a-bird class?

Oi.

But I went because I adore you.

And because I knew we'd make it ours.

Your painted swan was horrible. Mine was infinitely worse.

You told me as much, and we cracked up, laughing over our hideous swans.

And I love laughing with you.

That's how you made a wretched class fun.

You know what else is fun? Kissing you like crazy in Central Park.

We did that the next day in a do-over of one of the best dates I've ever had—swan boats.

The vendor did give us the evil eye when we put down our deposit, didn't he? Pretty sure he recognized us as the scofflaws we are. But so worth it. Because recreating that kiss with you in the middle of the lake on a swan boat was simply magic.

I get lost in your kisses. I forget about time and place and reason— everything but you.

Later, after we left the park, I forgot the world again when I took you to bed.

Something I always want to do with you.

I crave you, love you, adore you.

Let's toast to new date nights, and new places to vacation, and new awful classes that we have a blast taking, and messing up, and laughing at.

The world is ours to explore.

The day you decided to make me your sexy letter-writing partner-in-crime was the best day of my life.

Your Sexy (Sexiest!) Ex-Boyfriend

* * *

I flick the piece over to Matthew's inbox and write Summer back with one word.

Perfect.

When the clock strikes five, Bryn calls, demanding I meet her right away at Gin Joint.

I oblige, zipping over to Chelsea, finding my bestie waiting on a plush sapphire-blue lounge.

She pops up, grinning wildly, and I know why. She texted me a week ago when it happened, and now I get to gawk.

"Show me," I demand.

She flashes me her ring, a stunning emerald-cut diamond, gorgeous and so damn big. "They say size doesn't matter, but when it comes to diamonds and dicks, I say it does," I declare.

Bryn laughs deeply, pats my chest before wrapping me in a hug, and says, "And in friendship."

"Wait, are you saying the size of my boobs matters?"

"No, your heart, sweetie." Breaking the embrace, she taps my breastbone. "Your big, soft, mushy heart."

I let go, bring a finger to my lips, and say, "Shh. Don't tell anyone."

I grab a drink, and we catch up. She tells me everything about her vacation to Canada, and I tell her about dating Ransom, and when I ask when she's getting married, she says in the winter in Cancun.

"You're coming, right?" she asks.

"Destination wedding? I'm there."

"And you'll be with Ransom?"

I tense, all my muscles going tight. My throat is dry. Will I be with Ransom then? I hope so. But even if we're not, that won't change anything about my friendship with Bryn.

"I plan to. But I'll be there, with or without him."

The words come more easily than I could have imagined before taking a risk with Ransom. It feels right to say them.

More so, it feels right to believe them.

* * *

Later that night, Ransom comes over, and when I yank open the door, I feel different.

Freer.

Like a weight has been lifted.

Truth be told, the weight's been coming off for some time. Maybe the last of it is gone now. Or maybe voicing my certainty to Bryn made me take notice.

I pull him inside, needing to touch him, unable to resist him. I plant a hot, sensual kiss on his lips, sighing against him, savoring the taste of him.

When we break the kiss, he gives me a curious look. "You're in an interesting mood today."

I'm fluttery. I'm tingling. And I should feel nervous, but I don't. I'm ready to say the words filling up my heart.

"It's because I'm falling in love with you," I say, and

for a split second, I brace for the pain or the worry to slam into me.

Neither does.

Instead, Ransom smiles, slides a hand around my neck, and meets my gaze. "Oh, sunshine, I'm definitely already in love with you."

21

RANSOM

Christmas Eve

I'd be lying if I said I wasn't having flashbacks.

As I pick up the velvet box, weigh it in my hand, then slide it into my pocket, I remember the last time I did this.

There are moments when I think I must be insane to try it again.

But as soon as those thoughts land in my head, I brush them away. I'm not interested in the old mottos anymore. I don't cling to them for safety.

And I don't want them to trip me up.

If I'm insane, it's a good kind of crazy.

When I go to Teagan's home that night to spend Christmas Eve together, I stay in the moment.

And the moment includes kissing her, drinking hot chocolate, and listening to cheesy holiday music as snow falls outside her picturesque reading nook window.

Then it's time for stockings, and I tell her to grab the one I hung for her.

When she dips her hand inside and pulls out the box, she shoots me a curious look—a rather intrigued one.

My heart pounds against my ribs, thumping out a potent rhythm of hope.

Of second chances.

And most of all, of yeses.

"Ransom," she says, her voice choked with emotion.

And in a flash, I move in front of her and get down on one knee.

Hope floods me.

Nerves fill me.

And love guides me.

"Teagan King, the last six months with you have been wildly fun, incredibly sexy, intensely romantic, and filled with so much love that each day I wonder how it's possible to feel so much. But it must be, because it's happening." I stop to take a breath—there's so much more to say. "I want to spend all my days with you. I'm in love with you, and I love you, and I want to sing 'Summer Nights' with you and down chocolate milkshakes together and go out with our friends and play laser tag and stay in bed and curl up with each other. With you, only you, always you."

She brings her hand to her mouth, gasping as she nods vigorously and keeps nodding like she can't stop.

Like she's as thrilled, delighted, and absolutely happy as I am.

"I would love to marry you," she says, and I take the box and open it, then slide a diamond solitaire onto her ring finger, gazing at it and loving the way it looks on my fiancée.

This time, this love will last.

All the walls have come down. I've pushed past all my fears. And I'm stepping into a new future with the woman I want to spend the rest of my life with.

* * *

Two months later, we're in Cancun, happy as clams, ready for Logan to marry Bryn, knowing we'll be the next in our group to say our *I dos*. Yeah, all my single soldiers have fallen.

Fallen happily into their forevers.

22

LOGAN

February

Some things in life are easy, some are damn easy, and some are so easy you barely even have to think.

Choosing baseball over basketball? Simple.

Lining up for hours to source the perfect piece of kitty couture for Amelia to dress Queen LaTofu in? No question.

But this, right here, right now? Standing in front of the mirror and adjusting my bow tie before I speak the most important words I'll ever say in my life?

It's the simplest thing of all.

Because loving Bryn is easy.

It's never been hard. It's always been the most natural thing in the world. We fit together so damn well, and marrying the love of my life is the most honest thing I could do.

Because that's how we are together—we're honest with each other, all the damn time.

My heart was aligned with hers the moment we locked eyes over that Snoopy lunch box.

And I can't wait to make it official.

I give my bow tie one last tweak. Official indeed.

"Dad, did you know elephants are pregnant for nearly two years?"

I blink and turn to my daughter sitting on the hotel bed, her legs swinging back and forth against the white bedspread. "I did not know that."

"They are. And when they give birth, their entire herd gathers around to protect the mom and new baby from . . ." She pauses, taking her time with the next word. "Preda . . . pred-a-tors." She nods with the authority of an expert, which she just so happens to be. It takes a lot to beat Amelia at animal trivia.

"That's pretty smart of the pack to look out for the baby like that." I crouch down beside her and take her small hands in mine, meeting her eyes, trying to understand my little girl. Despite her mother remarrying, and despite Bryn and I having been together for almost two years, I need to make sure that this elephant diversion isn't due to any last-minute nerves on Amelia's part. "Sweetie pie, are you ready for today?"

She nods, zero indecision in her eyes. "Shouldn't I be asking you that?"

I grin. "Well, if you did, I'd answer that with a big yes. I am, indeed, ready to marry Bryn, and to do so with my brilliant and beautiful daughter standing by my side."

She gives me that cheeky little smile that melts me every time, and *this kid*. I'm so damn lucky to have her.

"Then I'm ready too. Also, I really want to have that cake."

"You and me both."

There's a rap on the door of the suite. "Knock, knock!" Bryn calls as she swings it open.

"Hey!" I spin around and cover my eyes before she can enter the room. "I'm not supposed to see you before the wedding."

"Well, face the window. I forgot my something blue."

"And you couldn't have Teagan get it for you?" But there's a smile on my lips. Because this is us—real and making our own rules. If things don't work, we change them—like Bryn did with her job, like I did in managing my time between my work, my daughter, and the woman I'm about to call my wife.

"My something blue is personal, thank you very much. And besides, my suitcase is a mess." I hear shuffling as Bryn riffles through her luggage, but I don't peek.

"I'm glad you're both here," Amelia says, sounding more sage than a nearly-nine-year-old should.

"Oh yeah? Why's that?" I ask, a smile in my voice.

"Because there's something I want to ask you."

The swish of material stops, and Bryn asks, "What can we do for you?"

"When are you going to have a baby?"

I stop breathing—I have to, the way my chest constricts.

What?

"Sorry, sweetie?" Bryn asks, apparently doubting her hearing as much as I am, because *what did Amelia just say?*

"Well, you two are getting married. And after people get married, they have babies. It's just what happens."

I finally find my voice. "It's not what happens with everyone."

"Yeah. It doesn't happen with everyone," Bryn echoes.

"It's what happened with Isla's mommies when they got married," Amelia responds, and the story of her bestie's new little brother does ring a bell. "And you guys already have me. I'd be a great help with a baby, just like Isla is."

"I know you would, sweetheart." I swallow around the golf-ball-sized lump in my throat.

"The best," Bryn agrees.

"So? Does that mean you'll have one soon?" Amelia presses, and I should call Oliver and tell him to recruit my daughter because she could put some serious pressure on a client. She'd be terrifying in a court of law.

Right now, thanks to this adorable interrogator, the bow tie around my neck has never felt tighter.

Bryn and I have discussed the possibility of children. Of course we have. You don't go from "Let's get naked" to "How 'bout we get married?" without some important stuff in between.

But when it comes to the question of kids, we'd agreed to table it. It wasn't a no—and it wasn't a yes. It was a "not now, but maybe someday" situation.

After all, Bryn adores Amelia. *I* adore Amelia. We

moved in together and planned a wedding, and that makes my heart full to bursting. Why would I push for anything more?

"Amelia, sweetheart, you would be an excellent big sister," Bryn starts, and her soft footsteps pad closer to the bed where my daughter sits. "But a marriage isn't about having babies. It's about commitment. It's about promising to love each other for the rest of our lives."

I peek through my fingers and out the window. Palm trees dance in the gentle breeze. Waves softly whisper to the shore. Attendants string flowers around the wire arch under which we'll say our vows in a few hours' time.

I've been looking forward to standing there for weeks. Months, even.

And Bryn's right. This day is about us, and the promise we'll make to each other in front of the people in our lives who do mean the most to us—including Amelia.

Especially Amelia.

But something about Bryn's words has me thinking. Before she came along, I didn't think I had room in my life to care for anyone like I did my daughter. Within days, my fiancée turned that notion on its head.

What if having another kid is like that? What if it's something I didn't know I needed but I've been missing all along?

"So, no babies for now," Amelia says, and I focus on my daughter and the here and now.

"Yes. No babies for now," Bryn agrees, her voice final.

Like there's no room for argument.

Like it's set in stone.

Her dress swishes again as she moves toward the door. "I should get back to the girls before they send out a search party."

"Yeah." I nod, my eyes still on that floral arch. "Can't wait to see you out there soon."

She leaves the room, and my last words to her feel true. I still cannot wait to marry this woman.

But it turns out there's a new elephant in the room, and the pack isn't so sure where they stand when it comes to giving birth.

"Wait." I spin around to go after her, but the door's already closed.

That's probably for the best. This isn't the time to start long conversations about when we should take the next step in our relationship. I should just focus on the wedding, and deal with this what-if later.

"You want me to go find her, Daddy?" Amelia asks.

Yes.

But no. Not now.

Instead, I launch myself at my daughter and wrap my arms around her in a big bear hug.

"How 'bout we spend some time just you and me before you go to hang out with the girls?" I reply, and as we play animal trivia and discuss Amelia's latest favorite books, I'm as present as I can be.

But all the while, her question replays in my mind.

When are you going to have a baby?

I thought I knew the answer, but it turns out, I don't.

And that conversation that should have been quite easy?

It's really damn difficult.

23

RANSOM

I am most definitely a mantra guy.

But I don't need a mantra to tell me this: My wife-to-be is an undeniable babe. Also, she owns both my heart and my dick, because both are enjoying the photo of her on my screen. The light-blue dress clings to her curves in a way that is almost indecent.

Almost.

After all, indecent wasn't the dress code for this afternoon's wedding.

Fitz gives a low, appreciative whistle as he sidles closer to me in the private bar area and glances at my phone. "No idea how such a hot babe wound up with you, Ransom."

"I could say the same thing about yourself."

"It's true. My man is hot AF," Fitz says just as Dean joins us and slides his arm around his husband's waist.

"You two are disgustingly in love," I say dryly.

"Just like you," Dean replies.

I raise my glass. "Madly and passionately. I am well and truly committed."

"Did someone say you need to be committed?"

I grin at the sound of Logan's voice and swivel my stool to face him and Oliver as they walk into the bar.

"Very funny." Fitz stands and rolls up the sleeves on his button-down shirt before opening his arms out wide. "C'mere, asshole. Give me your last hug as a free man."

"I'm getting married, not going to jail." Logan laughs and claps him on the back, then slides onto the stool next to mine as he signals to the bartender for a round of drinks.

But there's something slightly off about him. This doesn't seem like the same man who gave me a pep talk about marriage all those months ago in the park.

Interesting.

"Where's your lovely little lady?" Dean asks Logan.

"I just dropped Amelia off with the girls," Logan replies as the bartender places five beers in front of us and we raise them in a toast.

"To Logan, the man of the hour," I call out. "May you enjoy a long and happy marriage. And may said marriage not impede on your ability to commit to paintball or laser tag or kickball."

"Hear, hear," calls Fitz, and after our glasses clink together, Logan takes a sip.

A long sip.

Then another one.

"You okay there, man?" I ask, setting my beer on the counter.

"Yeah. Fine. I'm good." He nods. "I'm okay."

"You sure?" I narrow my brows.

He nods, but he doesn't meet my gaze. "Yeah. I'm fine."

"Do you think he's fine?" Oliver deadpans.

"I think he might not be fine," Dean replies. "But cut him some slack. It's not every day you get hitched."

"It's not." I shake my head, checking out the scene, kind of amazed. "Whoever thought this would happen? All of us studs, married or getting married."

"I, too, am amazed you've found someone to put up with you." Oliver needles me, but his eyes are on Logan.

Mine are too.

Is he simply a bit nervous? Maybe. He's been married once before. Perhaps he's worried that the second time around won't be a charm.

Nah. I dismiss the idea with another sip of beer. Logan's head over heels for Bryn. No way that could be it.

"Have you and Teagan set a wedding date yet?" Fitz asks me, changing the subject.

"This summer." My shoulders pull back a little in pride. "We want to have a baby soon, so we thought we should tie the knot first."

"Congrats, bro. Can't wait to meet the little Norths." Fitz holds out a fist to bump, and I meet it.

"How did you know that was what you wanted?" Logan asks, intensely serious.

I almost spit my beer across the counter. *What?*

"Dude, that's a little out of the blue." I laugh. "But to answer your question, we both want kids. Always have.

I love my sisters, and I'm super close to them, and Teagan wants a family too. We really want to start one together."

"And you aren't worried that it will disturb the balance of what you already have?" Logan asks, and a light goes on in my head.

Ding-ding-ding.

We have a winner.

Logan wants another kid.

Or maybe Bryn does.

Shit!

Or maybe they're already pregnant.

That's it. It has to be it. What else could have him so tied up in knots on a day I know he's been itching for?

Next to me, Oliver's phone buzzes, and he peers at a text.

His eyes spark, then he says, "I need to nip up to my room. Grab something Summer needs. Be right back."

He drains the last of his beer and slips his cell into his pocket, then takes off for the elevator bank like there's a herd of wildebeests on his tail.

I chat with the guys some more, but Logan still seems out of sorts.

I flash back again to Fitz's wedding, to the day when Logan gave me those frank words—words I needed to hear.

Maybe he needs the same—a friend to give it to him straight.

I clap my hand on his shoulder. "You're a lucky guy. And whatever's on your mind right now, I know you and Bryn will work it out. You're going to be a great husband."

"Thanks. Appreciate it."

I lean closer, speaking quietly, "You're a great dad too."

He gives me a grateful nod. "Thanks. That means a lot."

I shrug. "I'm only saying it because it's true."

As we finish our beers, I hope that my words give him the comfort and confidence he needs.

Just as he did for me several months ago.

Because that's what friends do.

24

SUMMER

There's no shame in ogling my husband.

Not as he's coming out of the pool, those tight Speedos clinging to every bit of his body and revealing everything—and I do mean *everything*.

Not as he steps out of the shower in the morning.

And certainly not an hour before the wedding when he steps out of the elevator in that white button-down shirt and those pressed tan pants, his eyes screaming *sex*.

"You wanted me?" he asks, gesturing to his phone.

"I do. It's an emergency so important I had to have you meet me here." My eyes lust over his face then his body as the doors close behind him.

"What kind of emergency?" He slips the phone away and steps closer, a playful look in his eyes. "Whatever could you possibly need?"

I grab his hand and yank him toward our hotel room. "You."

And thank the Lord for vacations and this perfect

man of mine, because a midday O should be on every wife's wish list.

"What brought that on?" Oliver asks a satisfying length of time later as he buttons up his fly. "Not that I'm complaining. I will never, ever complain about pre-wedding sex. Or any sex with you, for that matter."

I shrug. "Can't a woman just enjoy her husband's body every now and then?"

"Absolutely she can. In fact, if we ever do a vow renewal, we should include it as part of the official contract."

"Thou shalt have sex whenever thy wife wishes." I wrap my arms around his neck and try to comb his just-fucked hair into submission.

"Thou shalt deliver multiple Os to thy wife whenever and wherever thou can," he murmurs, and his mouth glides over mine in a kiss that I feel everywhere —my lips, my chest, then lower between my legs.

But before I can lose myself in contemplation of round two, I take his hand and use all my willpower to walk us back out into the corridor so we can support our friends before their special moment.

"How's Logan?" I ask as we stroll along the hall. "I don't think I've ever seen a man as excited to get married as he is."

"Hey! I'll have you know I was desperate to put a ring on your finger."

"Present company excluded, of course."

"Of course." He stops and pulls me close, our bodies flush. But his eyes cloud over, and he bites down on his lip.

"What is it?"

He glances toward Bryn's door, three rooms down from where we stand, then back to me. "Does Bryn seem okay to you?"

"Okay?" What's he talking about?

"Has she been sick perhaps?" He clicks his fingers together. "Drinking. Did she have any cocktails at dinner last night?"

I shake my head. "She wanted to avoid a hangover."

"Has she had any wine this morning at all, then? Some champagne perhaps?"

"No. But it's barely twelve." I step back and fold my arms across my chest. "What's going on with you, Oliver?"

He winces. "It's not what's going on with me. It's what's going on with them."

I wave my hand, encouraging him to continue. "Out with it, lover."

He takes a deep breath. "Look, Logan said something, and . . . I think they might be pregnant."

"Pregnant?" I widen my eyes. Could that be true?

I mean, technically, of course it could. And while Bryn has told me that they're not looking to expand their family any time soon, I do understand that a penis plus a vagina can equal babies, even with protection.

But the odds seem so slim.

That's how I've always felt when it came to Oliver and me—we use protection, and so we're safe. I'm on the pill. We won't end up pregnant.

"Summer?" Oliver steps closer again and places his hands on my shoulders.

"Sorry. Lost in thought." I dismiss the idea and focus on the issue at hand. "Actually, come to think of it, Bryn did look a little pale this morning after she came back from Logan's room."

"Logan's room?"

"She said she had to get something from her luggage . . ." But the bride wasn't supposed to see the groom before the wedding. What if that wasn't where she went at all? What if she was worried that the walls of her hotel room would be an ineffective barrier when it came to hiding her morning sickness from her two best friends?

"Wow! I mean, that's amazing news. I can't wait to congratulate them," I finally say, and I mean it. I'm thrilled that a baby is in the cards for these two people who are simply head over heels for each other, and who already ace the parenting game.

Oliver nods. "Logan's an amazing dad, and Bryn is great with Amelia. They'll be perfect."

"They really will." I grin. "Oh, I am going to buy the cutest little onesies for their bub! And socks. Baby socks are so sweet!"

"Baby socks?" Oliver laughs. "I did not know of your penchant for small footwear."

"Well, let me tell you that baby socks are some of the teensiest, tiniest, cutest clothing items known to man." I nod, then pause. "But I guess this means they won't be coming to Costa Rica with us in the summer."

Oliver frowns. "No. Probably not."

Down the hall, a door swings open. A couple walks toward us, his arm tight around her waist. They can't seem to tear their eyes off each other, and clearly she hasn't bothered to hide the just-fucked hair on her man —he's wearing it loud and proud, like he wants to proclaim their recent rendezvous to the world.

"They look like us," Oliver whispers in my ear as the elevator dings and they step inside.

"They do. I'm sure we've looked like that on so many of our vacations," I say, but my mind is a whir, like the reels on a slot machine. "Can we talk seriously for a moment?"

Oliver glances up and down the now empty hall. "Here?"

I grab his hand, lead him to our room, and pull my key card from my pocket—because what could improve a hot AF dress more than pockets?—and slide it over the keypad.

Oliver slips in beside me, and we walk out to the balcony, where the fresh sea air washes over me like a balm—always moving and free.

"Are you okay?" He presses a hand to the bare skin above the low back of my dress.

"Yes." I turn to face him. "Look, Logan and Bryn getting pregnant has me thinking."

"Oh." He nods, and I rush to shake my head before he gets the wrong idea.

"I know we've spoken before about having babies, and we said we didn't want them just now." I take a deep breath. Here goes nothing. "But I don't think I want them . . . ever."

I search Oliver's face for some sign—some indication that this is either the best or worst news he's heard all morning.

He's blank as a stone.

I take a deep breath and continue. "I just . . . I love our life. I love our dates and our time together and our vacations. I love you, and you and me—"

"And our impromptu midday sex?" A twinkle sparks in his eyes.

"I absolutely love our impromptu midday sex," I agree. "And I love children. I adore Amelia, and I'm sure I'll love playing Auntie Summer to Logan and Bryn's new little one whenever he or she comes along too. But as long as you're on the same page as me, I would be completely okay with not having children for the rest of our lives."

Oliver grins. "I would be more than okay with that." He places a hand under my chin, tilting my face up until just a whisper and a kiss separate our lips. "I have everything I need with you." He kisses my lips, his leg wedged between mine, our arms wrapped around each other, and it feels so right. I love this—I love us. And I definitely don't feel the need to add a child to an already perfect cocktail of life.

Oliver's phone vibrates against my thigh. I groan against his mouth.

"It can't be that important." He kisses me again, but when the vibrating continues, I pull back.

He fishes the cell from his pocket. "It's Logan. I should probably go."

"Same." I peer at the wall as if I can see right through

to Bryn's room a few doors down. "It's nearly ceremony time."

"See you out there, cupcake." Oliver kisses me once more, and we go our separate ways, but as I walk, my steps are somehow lighter. Maybe that was a decision I didn't know I needed to make until now, but it most definitely feels like the right one.

I knock on the door to Bryn's suite, and when she opens it, the sight steals my breath. *Wow.*

"Do I look okay?" Bryn runs her hands down the sides of the white gown that hugs the top half of her body and descends into some kind of flowing magic at the bottom. It's sexy yet sweet, beachy yet bombshell—perfect for a Cancun wedding.

"*Okay?*" I echo. "You put the *A* in amazing. Logan is going to lose his mind."

"I hope so." She smiles, and I step inside and close the door behind me.

I wave to Teagan and Amelia on the balcony, then turn back to the woman who has become one of my closest friends in the entire world. Perhaps it's good that the others are outside—there are only ten minutes until we need to go downstairs, but this will give us time to chat.

And from the look in Bryn's eyes, I think we need to do that.

"Bryn, sweetie, is everything okay?" I ask.

"It is." She takes a deep breath. "I'm marrying the man of my dreams."

"I know. But you seem kind of . . . distant this morning," I say, easing into the subject gently. If she doesn't want to tell me, I'm not going to press.

"You noticed, huh?" She heaves a sigh and walks over to the chaise lounge by the window, resting her hands on the frame. "Honestly, this is eating me up. I need to tell you something about Logan and me." She glances out at Amelia and Teagan, then back to meet my gaze. "It's about having a baby."

I can't hold back anymore. "Congratulations!" I squee and rush to hug her. "This is the best news!"

"Pardon?" she asks, and I pull away so I can see her face and the excitement I know must be there.

"Sorry—Oliver told me. I guess Logan must have told him," I say, grinning like a fool.

"Told him what exactly?" Bryn steps back and folds her arms, and uh-oh. This doesn't look like the face of a woman about to confess her glowing-with-child status.

"About . . . you being pregnant," I say, but as Bryn's eyebrows draw into an even deeper frown, I know without question—

She is not having a baby.

And that means the boys have the wrong end of the stick.

25

BRYN

From the moment I saw the dress, I knew.

This was it.

This was the outfit I would wear when I married the love of my life.

But as I run my hands over the silky material that falls around my legs, I feel an uncertainty.

Of course, not about marrying Logan. That's a no-brainer.

I don't need to read an article like "Five Hints You're Marrying the Love of Your Life." I could write that piece myself, along with some companion posts like "Do You Really Know When You Think You Know?" (hint: the answer is yes) and "When 'I Do' Is All Too True."

No, this uncertainty stems from something else entirely.

"I see Daddy!" Amelia whispers excitedly, her eyes glued to the gap in the door that leads to the white sand

and floral arch where our friends and family wait. "Do you want to see him, Bryn?"

I smile and kneel behind her, giving her shoulder a squeeze. "I think I'll wait until we walk down the aisle."

"O-kaa-aay." Amelia doesn't sound particularly confident in my choice as she singsongs three syllables into the two-syllable word. "But he looks very handsome."

I laugh. "I'm sure he does."

Another thing I have no doubt about.

But this whole baby situation? That's another matter entirely. It's thrown me for a loop.

I'd been so happy with the plan to wait a few years before trying for a baby. Logan and I both manage our own businesses, and with mine so new, it didn't seem smart to add a baby to the mix too early. Not only that, but we have this gorgeous girl in front of me—the only member of our bridal party because she's the only one we need, in more ways than one.

Not yet. Two words I'd felt so confident about.

But Amelia's question this morning made me realize something. I'm on the brink of marrying the man I love madly. I don't think I want to wait to try for a baby. Why should we delay? We don't live in a world where I have to choose whether to be a wife or a businesswoman or a mother. I can be anything and everything. I want it all, and I want it now. I want what the guys think I already have – a baby in my belly.

"Bryn, we're ready to go whenever you are. Just say the word." Maria, the event planner, nods toward the closed doors.

"Great. Let's do it."

Maria hands me the bouquet of tropical flowers as I stand and thank her. I breathe in the heady aroma of the beautiful blooms, centering myself in this moment.

I am about to marry the man I love most.

My what-if guy who isn't a what-if, but an only-and-forever.

"Let's do this." I press a quick kiss to Amelia's soft hair, and Maria says a few words into her headset as the music starts to play.

The doors open, and Amelia focuses on the aisle ahead like a true professional. But just before she takes a step, she spins, runs to my side, and plasters her tiny arms around my waist, her basket of flowers gently tapping my thighs.

"I love you," she whispers.

She loves me.

My ovaries melt into a thousand tiny love puddles.

"I love you too," I whisper, and she gives me another squeeze, then pulls away, faces the guests, and scatters petals as she walks toward them.

Tears prick my eyes, and I blink them back, focusing on the orchids in my bouquet, then look up again to see a pair of deep, sensual eyes staring at me from underneath that floral arch. Logan lights up my body even from a distance, and a shiver runs through me.

Butterflies flit in my stomach, but not from nerves. They're gliding on wings of excitement. I cannot wait to do this—to walk down the aisle and marry the man I love. In fact, I want this so badly I could run.

The sand is soft between my toes as I move quickly

past our friends and family. Fitz with his arm wrapped around Dean. Summer with her fingers twined tightly with Oliver's. And Ransom and Teagan, his arm around her waist, holding her close.

I pass my bouquet to Teagan in the front row and rush to my fiancé's side, and because he is so darn kissable, I press my lips to his. He slinks his arms around my waist, kissing me back like nobody's watching.

"You look amazing," he whispers before dotting one last kiss onto my cheek.

Heat flushes my neck. "Thank you. You look amazing too."

What would he look like holding a newborn baby in his arms? And not in five or ten years, when we're a little older, a little more tired—what would he look like if we had one right now?

I already know the answer.

He'd look like the perfect man he already is—the perfect man for me.

"Are you two ready?" the officiant asks in a low voice, her gaze darting between us.

"So ready," Logan says, and I open my mouth to agree.

But I can't.

Not just yet. Not with these thoughts of babies and family swimming in my brain, making it hard to focus on the moment.

We're a team in everything we do, and I want to start my marriage the way I intend to live it—with complete transparency. Not mentioning details has gotten us into trouble before, and I won't let it hinder things again.

I take a deep breath. Can I really do this? Can I really delay my own wedding and tell this man I want it all, and I want it now?

I hold up my pointer finger to the celebrant. "Can you please give us one minute?"

26

LOGAN

Universal truth: no man ever wants his wedding delayed.

But since the woman who's just held up her hand to slow the proceedings is the most important one in the world to me, I don't say a word, even when the officiant widens her eyes, even when I hear a low whistle from someone in the crowd.

Bryn pulls me over to the shade of a nearby palm, and I cup her cheek and pull her close, a bemused smile twisting my lips. "Is everything okay?"

"Yes." She shakes her head, an adorable wrinkle creasing her brow. "No. Amelia's question this morning about babies, and then Summer and Oliver thinking we're pregnant, and—"

"They think we're pregnant?"

"Not anymore. But all those things had *me* thinking, and I want to marry you today, and I absolutely want to do it regardless, but I need to know something first." She searches my eyes, so honest, so beautiful. "When it comes to having another baby, do you still think it's something we should look at in a few years' time? Because I did, but I don't want to wait anymore. I really want this now."

Wow.

I hadn't expected that.

Just when I thought it was impossible to fall any more in love with her, I do.

In fact, it's all I can do not to wrap her in my arms, throw her over my shoulder, and take her up to our hotel room, caveman-style, to get started on her proposition right away.

"Bryn, my heart is so full when I'm with you." I graze my thumb over the soft skin of her cheek. "And I would love to start growing our family whenever you feel ready, whether that's in two years, two months, or two hours. I want to do it all with you, Bryn. Everything."

She gives me a sexy little smile. "Should we make a baby together, Mr. Smolder?"

"Yes. Yes, we absolutely should." I sweep my hand around the back of her neck and pull her in for a whirlwind of a kiss. I kiss her like she's my forever, and my wife, and a mother to my child, and the mother of our future children—because she's all those things to me and more.

Someone catcalls from the crowd, and she pulls back, a sexy flush to her cheeks. I love putting that flush there.

I can't stop my grin. "Is there anything else? Or should we go and get married?"

"Let's do it." She smiles, and we walk back to the officiant, who soon pronounces us husband and wife.

Forever.

Later on, after we dance the night away with our family and friends, we make good on our commitment. I strip off her dress to reveal her lacy blue lingerie, and I make love to my wife again and again and again.

Three months later, we learn we're pregnant, and eight months after that, we welcome our second daughter into the world. We name her Ashlee, after Bryn's mom.

And from the moment I see her sweet little face, I fall in love all over again—with our daughters and the woman who made me believe in love again.

A LITTLE EPILOGUE

Ransom

But wait. Whatever did happen to my sister and Martinez? Was it as simple as an auction bid? Is falling for someone ever simple?

Never.

Let's hear it from them though as we go back in time to the auction.

THE STORY OF TEMPEST AND MARTINEZ

AN EXTRA SPECIAL EPILOGUE

Tempest

The afternoon of the auction . . .

So it's a Saturday afternoon, I'm hanging at my brother's Murray Hill pad, reviewing a column I've written on the best ways to avoid hidden fees in mutual funds, when a solar eclipse occurs.

The sun, moon, and earth align.

Metaphorically.

First, an email lands in my inbox from my lit agent, Viviana Grayson.

Tempest!

Guess who just earned a bonus for her German edition of The

Girl's Guide to Personal Finances? It's also my favorite kind of bonus.

The big, huge kind with lots of zeroes.

They love you in Germany.

And Korea. Check coming from there.

And Hungary. Yet another check.

And Brazil. One more check.

I'll be sending you royalty checks from all those territories this weekend. Click on the PDF to see the amounts.

Xoxo
Viv

Naturally, I click that PDF so fast my finger hits a new land speed record.

I blink.

Blink again.

Enlarge the PDF.

I mean, I do wear glasses. So I might be seeing it wrong.

But that is a hella lot of zeroes.

Like, five zeroes.

And I write back to Viviana with a series of fireworks GIFs because I'm not entirely sure what else to say.

Except *Thanks for being the badass you are.*

So I add that and hit send.

Then my brother jerks around, fiddling with his bow tie. "Temp, you don't think Martinez is hot, do you?"

The last name rings a vague bell.

Just to get his goat, since his goat needs to be gotten, I furrow my brow. "Who's that? An actor on *Scrubs?*"

He rolls his eyes. Something he does with me so frequently I sometimes worry they might get stuck in the back of his head.

"*Scrubs* has been off the air for years. Good job, Ms. Anti Pop Culture."

I point out how well I know Broadway as he explains that Martinez is the guy he's always referring to as Marty Boy, which is why I rarely hear his full name.

Then he says it.

Adrian Martinez.

And does that ever ring a bell.

That rings all the tingly bells indeed.

But it's nice to mess with my brother.

With lightning speed, I turn to my best friend, Google, and look up "Adrian Martinez." *The* Adrian Martinez with the dark blond hair that has such a delicious swoop to it. The one with those crystal blue eyes, and with that jawline—it's statue-worthy.

He's the guy.

I met him two days ago.

I'm not simply talking about walking past the Times Square billboard. Though he's hard to look away from there in his briefs, plastered over ten stories of New York skyscraper.

I'd like to count my royalties over the grooves of his abs.

With my tongue.

"Why didn't you tell me *your* Martinez was Adrian Alejandro Martinez from the Gigante underwear ad in Times Square?"

And from earlier in the week during an interview.

Only, I can't let Ransom know. Not yet, at least. That would give my brother too much fodder and too much ire. He's more protective than he needs to be, but this girl makes her own choices. I close my laptop, rearranging my face to be expressionless so he doesn't see right through me.

I'm good at that—presenting a poker face to the world if I have to.

But still, I kind of can't believe this is him.

A guy my brother knows. A guy my brother smack-talks with. A guy who's going to the player's auction tonight.

Sometimes the world works in mysterious ways.

Or perhaps intentional ones.

Because I know what I want, and I think I know how to get it.

* * *

Ransom

. . .

Hmmm. I'm thinking they met before the auction now. I have a sneaking suspicion that somehow they crossed paths.

Let's go back a few more days.

Time to rewind.

* * *

Martinez

Earlier that week, a few days before the auction

When I come into the ninth inning of a game, whether the bases are loaded or empty, nothing distracts me.

I wear blinders because that's my motherfucking job.

To drown out the noise of the crowd, the game, the day, the night.

Nothing else matters.

I take to the field, head to the mound, and enter the zone.

It's a skill I've mastered, and I use it in other areas of my life too.

When I'm reading a book in the park, when I go to a museum, or when I have dinner with friends—I ignore everything else and am present in the moment.

That's why it's killing me when I sit down for an

interview in a quiet coffee shop with a reporter from a lifestyle site who wants to do a feature on me.

"Devon Patrick." The sandy-haired reporter interviewing me introduces himself, then gestures to a brunette with electric-blue glasses, pretty pink lips, and a gorgeous smile.

"Tempest," she says, holding out a hand. "I'll be here to sign for Devon."

I'd been told by my publicist that an ASL interpreter would be here for the reporter. "Adrian Alejandro Martinez," I say to both of them, then to her, I add, "Charmed."

Because I am. She's beguiling to look at.

Which means I need to apply the same focus to Devon that I would to a save situation.

The bases are loaded. There are no outs. The opposing team's top slugger's at the plate. I come in. Mow down the side.

The reporter begins with some standard questions, wanting to know when I moved to America, how many other languages I speak, if I go back to Europe often since I grew up in Spain, spent some time with family in Italy and visited grandparents frequently in France as a child.

I give him the answers that are widely known— when I was fourteen, Spanish, Italian, English and passable French thanks to my father's mother, and . . . as often as I can.

Tempest signs all my answers for him then translates his questions for me.

Sure, I'm talking to him, but I can't help but feel that

I'm talking to her too. He says something to her with his hands, and then she translates for me. "Adrian, tell us about growing up mostly in Spain, since it isn't widely known for baseball. Was that hard?"

"It came with its challenges, but I had great coaches and was determined to play in the Major Leagues," I say.

She smiles then tells Devon what I said.

"And you're close with your family?" he asks through her.

I nod, meeting his eyes as I answer, but I want to look at her, not only because I'm distracted by her soulful eyes and a smile I can't seem to get enough of.

I tell myself she's simply a woman I'm meeting as part of my job.

That I shouldn't be so taken with her so soon.

And I'm not truly taken, I suppose.

Yet I want to keep talking to her. Or, really, through her.

"I see my mother and father every week if I can. They live just outside the city. I have them over for dinner when I'm able to and when I'm not playing."

"What do you like to cook?" she blurts out, then she shakes her head, apologizes, and turns to Devon, signing quickly.

He chuckles, saying something to her silently with his hands.

She dips her head, then raises it, that smile curving her lips in an *oops, did I really say that* grin.

"I make a mean gazpacho. Paella, of course too. My father taught me how to make those. My mother is Italian and she loves classic Italian dishes. And, my grandmother in Paris made sure I knew how to make tarte normande. But I can't have those too often," I say, patting my belly and wiggling my eyebrows.

She grins. "It's always good to make sure you can do the Gigante ads," she says. Her fingers were flying as I spoke, and she signs her own comment as well, making the reporter chuckle again. I just get a kick out of the fact that she's seen my ads.

"But I also like to bake pizza," I add with a smile.

Devon grins, waiting for Tempest to translate. She does, and he replies through Tempest, "Pizza is life."

"From your mouth to God's ears," I say, tapping my chest then pointing in the air, glancing skyward.

Devon signs something else, then Tempest looks at me, those brown eyes locking with mine and once more distracting me.

Get in the zone, man.

"What kind of pizza do you bake?"

"I make a mean artichoke, sausage, and tomato pizza," I say wryly.

She licks her lips, mouths *Yum*, then repeats it to Devon.

"'Sounds delish,' he says," she tells me.

"The cheese melts on your tongue. The dough is pillowy. The tastes are incredible. *E come il paradiso nella boca*," I reply, dropping into Italian to say *it's like heaven in your mouth* because I can't help myself with this lovely woman who's so unexpectedly captivating.

"Sounds like it must be," she says and signs too.

Devon segues to other questions.

"Rumor has it you're a cat person," she relays. "I love cats," she adds to both of us.

The reporter shakes his head then pants like a dog.

"Dog person?" I ask him with a grin.

"Yes, he's a dog person," Tempest tells me.

"Personally, I love the feline attitude," I say, returning to the implied question about my pet preference. "I appreciate that take-it-or-leave-it vibe. You don't always know where you stand with a cat. I love that you must work for it with them." My attention keeps sliding to Tempest as she interprets my answer, but hey, she's the fellow cat lover. "Do you have cats?" I ask her.

After she signs the last thing, a smile takes over her face as if she's pleased that I asked her a question.

Devon chuckles and says something in sign language to her that she answers before turning her smiling gaze my way and telling me, "I have one. A tomcat. His name is—wait for it—Tom."

I laugh deeply. "I love the simplicity of that, Tempest."

She looks to Devon again for his next question. He fires it off, and she puts it to me. "What do you like to do for fun?"

"I enjoy cooking, Scrabble, and candlelit dinners," I say with a straight face.

She laughs, her hands whipping through my reply.

Devon arches a brow at me, mouthing *Really?* Then he says something to her.

"'Is that a line?' he wants to know," she says to me, laughing again as she poses the question.

I act deeply affronted, bringing my hand over my heart. "It's all true."

When the interview ends, I thank Devon, then I turn to ask the interpreter for her full name.

"Tempest North."

North.

It's not an uncommon name.

But it's not the most common either.

"I hope we will meet again," I say, because I'm a gentleman, and it's polite to establish one's intentions before asking for a phone number. But before I can, her phone trills.

She grabs it, checks the screen, then says she has to take it. She signs something to Devon, who nods, and then gives me a quick goodbye wave before they leave the shop together.

I sigh, shrugging. "What can you do?"

But as I make my way out of the café, I keep wondering if, with that surname, she's related to my friend.

And whether I have the guts to ask him.

* * *

When Saturday night rolls around, I decide to quiz Ransom after the fundraiser ends. But it turns out I don't need to.

Because the next time I hear the name Tempest North, it's when I learn that she was the bidder on the phone during my turn at the auction.

And she's won a date with me.

* * *

Tempest

The night of the auction

I'm due at the theater at seven thirty for an eight o'clock curtain. As soon as Ransom slides into his Lyft, I turn to my trusty companion.

My phone.

As I march to the theater district, I search for the details on the auction tonight.

The names of the players.

How it works.

And what to do if you can't be there.

As I cross Fifth Avenue, I learn you can buy a virtual ticket. And you can place a virtual bid. And you can set your bidding limits.

I flash back to Thursday.

To randomly meeting the Yankees pitcher, to that crackle of connection I felt with him, and to that moment at the end.

When I was sure he was asking for my number, for a way to reach out and see me again.

But then I had to dash.

Now, I've learned that guy is Marty Boy—my brother's friend—and he's going to be up for auction tonight, a date with him going to the highest bidder.

I draw a deep breath, letting it fuel this crazy decision.

I reach another crosswalk and stop to wait at the light.

I have the money. That email from my agent made it damn clear I have plenty to spend.

And it goes to a good cause—his charity of choice supports athletic programs for disadvantaged youth.

Why shouldn't I do this?

Why the hell not?

It's been a while since I met someone I clicked with. As in, years. Most men I meet are flummoxed by my twin careers—they don't know what to make of them or how to accommodate my crazy schedule. I'm either feverishly penning columns and books, studying the market, or prepping to interpret. It's hard to make time for a date, let alone for browsing the apps trying to meet someone.

This seems like going from zero to sixty on the find-a-date highway, but if there was ever a time to go for it, it's now.

I felt the chemistry, the connection.

I fill out the form, consider what I'd be willing to spend, and enter the numbers.

Then I add another zero.

There. Done. I turn my phone off, drop it in my purse, and ignore it until Hamilton dies.

As I make my way out of the theater, I turn on my phone, and a message blares at me from the auction organizers.

A burst of excitement flares inside my chest.

I hold my breath as I click open the text, hoping it's good news.

You've won a date with Adrian Martinez.

It's the *best* of news.
   And I can't wait.

* * *

Martinez

A few days later

The door to the bullpen swings open, and I jog across the field, wiggling my hand in my well-worn glove then adjusting the bill of my cap, as is my custom.

When I reach the pitcher's mound, the music crests, the crowd roars, and I nod to Jose Carnale, who's waiting there, his mask pushed back from his face.

We go over the pitches for the guy at the plate— Baltimore's slugger has been belting homers all season, not to mention plenty of doubles that send runners home. With a man on second, another on first, and only one run keeping us ahead, there is no room for error.

No room to let the runners move around the bases.

"Get 'em with the cutter," he says, then claps me on the back and trots to home plate.

I inhale deeply and visualize my ninety-eight-miles-per-hour cut fastball whizzing across the plate, teasing the batter and making him think it'll be straight down the middle.

But it'll veer to the outside corner, breaking at just the last second.

As I go into the windup, then throw the first pitch, it breaks beautifully, tricking the batter in a futile swing.

And that's how it goes for all three batters.

The first one strikes out looking, the next swinging, and the third pops up a lazy fly ball to first.

I record my thirtieth save of the season, we wrap up the home stand, and I eventually shower and make my way out of the stadium, finding my driver easily and heading away from the Bronx. But I don't go to my home off of Park Avenue.

Instead, I stop at a quiet restaurant in the East Nineties, a ramen joint that's up a flight of stairs and around a corner. The type of place with so many dark nooks it might as well invest in them.

Once I'm there, the hostess shows me to a quiet corner table, and my pulse spikes when I see the brunette with the blue glasses.

Spikes so much higher and faster than when I'm on the mound.

Tempest rises, smiles, and says, "Nice save, Tree."

"Nice job watching my game," I say, then slide a hand around her waist, my fingers skimming over her lower back.

She murmurs, slinking closer to me. "Who said I watched it? Maybe I just looked up the stats online to impress you."

I grin, yanking her closer, her firm, lush body pressed against mine. "I'm impressed, then. So very impressed, *mi querida.*"

She trembles as I call her my darling. "Fine, maybe I did watch. Also, I love when you talk to me in other languages."

I tuck a finger under her chin, lifting her face so our eyes meet. "Then I'll keep doing it. But first did you enjoy what you saw when you watched me?"

"A little. I think maybe I enjoy the feel of you a little more."

I shake my head in admiration. This woman. Her appetite. It matches mine perfectly.

That I discovered earlier this week when we met for lunch after she won me. The meal was good. The dessert of her was even better.

I experienced it again the next day when we met in the park and walked for an hour, talking about pizza and cats and New York and growing up mostly in Spain, a bit in Italy, and now and then in France, as well as her family and her fascinating careers , then decided being horizontal would be more fun than being upright.

And it was. Oh hell, yes, it was.

Now I have the distinct feeling she wants that again.

"Tempest, are you trying to distract me from eating?"

Her lips curve into a naughty grin. "Oh, no. I don't want to distract you from eating at all."

"So deliciously dirty," I tell her, then, in the middle of the tiny hole-in-the-wall restaurant, I haul her in for a kiss. I gather her close, bend my knees, since she's a little shorter, and brush my lips against hers.

It starts chastely, as far as kisses go with women you already adore.

But it doesn't stay chaste for long.

She loops her arms around my neck. I wrap mine tighter around her waist, and I draw her snug against me, all while kissing her more deeply, more passionately, with more tongue and teeth and fire.

She's heating me up with her sexy sighs, her soft skin, and the way she melts into my touch, her body liquid against mine.

When I break the kiss, she nibbles on the corner of her lips. "Hungry?"

"I am ravenous," I tell her.

We head to the hostess stand, place an order for delivery, and then book it to my place a few blocks away.

Once inside my penthouse, I press her against the wall.

"*Cuore mio*," I whisper. "Italian for *my heart.* I thought about you all day, *cuore mio.*"

"Not while you were on the mound in the ninth," she says, grabbing at my shirt and tugging it over my head.

"Fine, not then. You caught me on a technicality," I say, stripping off her skirt then pulling at her shirt. "But the rest of the day."

"All day? That's a long time to be thinking of me."

I growl, reach for her wrists, and pin them over her

head. I slam my pelvis against her, letting her feel the length of me, the truth of my desire for her. "Does it feel like I'm lying?"

She groans, shaking her head. "No, but you can show me the proof just to be sure."

And I do just that. Unhooking her bra. Tugging off her panties.

Finding a condom and then fucking her.

Hard, beautifully, and passionately up against the wall.

"So fucking gorgeous," I groan.

"Harder, more," she urges.

"And so greedy, *mi querida*. So greedy when you want my cock . . . deep in you."

"I do, oh God, I do," she murmurs as I thrust deeper, stroke faster, and slide my fingers between her legs and over that delicious rise of her, where she wants me the most.

"Oh, yes you do, and you'll get it. I'll make you come so damn hard."

A minute later, she's crying out, shouting, babbling, groaning as she comes apart.

And I follow her there, shuddering, cursing as an orgasm wracks my body.

After we clean up, I take her in my arms and ask her to spend the night.

She says yes.

* * *

The next night, after Fitz's wedding, she meets me here too, and we do it again and again and again.

As she curls up beside me in bed after midnight, she says, "I should tell my brother about us."

"Yes, you should tell him you won me and had to have me. And now I have to have you over and over."

"Is that what I should say?" she asks with a sassy lift of her brow.

"Maybe not *all* that," I tease, running my fingers down her waist. "But we should let him know I'll be seeing you as much as I possibly can—it seems I'm already addicted to you."

"And you haven't even had your official date with me yet," she says.

I shrug happily, draw her close, and drop a kiss onto her forehead. "When you know, you know."

And I know that there's something between us.

* * *

A few days later, we go on a double date, of all things.

We take pictures for social media. We tag each other and offer cute write-ups about the auction and the charities, snapping pictures as we walk through the Museum of Natural History, then watch a sunset in the park and drink milkshakes.

At the end of the night, as the four of us wander through the park, I fall back with Ransom while Teagan and Tempest move ahead. "Don't think for a second this changes anything between you and me."

The hockey star scoffs. "It changes nothing, asshole."

"Not a damn thing, you ugly bastard."

Hearing us, Tempest shrugs, and Teagan laughs, saying, "Boys will be boys."

And that's fine by me.

Then I say to my buddy, "By the way, about that bet . . . I'm glad you won."

He shoots me a look. "You are? Even though you had to pay up?"

"Crazy, I know. But I could tell you liked her. I could tell you wanted to be with her." I shrug. "Maybe you needed a little competitive nudge."

"Maybe I did," he says. "Thanks for giving it to me. She's pretty amazing."

"She is, and don't you ever lose sight of that."

"I'll do my best. Also, asshole, same for you with my sister."

"Don't worry, Puck Boy. I'll take good care of the woman I'm already falling in love with."

Ransom offers a fist for knocking, and I knock back.

Life is very, very good.

I'd like to tell that reporter that it's only gotten better since the day he interviewed me.

Especially since later that night when we're alone, she loops her arms around me, and asks if I can dirty talk to her in French too.

"*Mais oui, mon cheri.*"

And then I slide into that language, tell her all the filthy things I'll do to her, then show her too.

Soon after that, I say something else. Something sweet, rather than dirty.

Tempest, je t'aime.

Which I plan on saying in every language.

* * *

Ransom

Look, all I'm saying is I had a feeling.
   And I was right.
   So there.

EPILOGUE

Ransom

A year later

When the season ends with a gorgeous Stanley Cup in my hands, I think my life can't get better.

Because really, this is the motherfucking tops.

This is what I've played my ass off for my whole life over.

This chance.

This victory.

This Cup.

And it is awesome.

It is magic and moonlight and everything good in the world.

Plus, the Yankees are having a killer start to the season and that makes my sister all kinds of happy.

January and you can preorder it everywhere! Check out the prologue below!

Prologue

I don't have to see something to believe it. Don't have to experience something to know I'd like it.

I've never vacationed in Fiji, for instance, but I'm 100 percent confident I'd love every second in that tropical paradise.

I don't need to have tossed out the ceremonial first pitch at Dodger Stadium to know that it would be an all-time highlight if I did.

And there's one more thing.

I don't need to have had great sex to know I'd love it.

I'm confident I'd absolutely, completely fucking adore, worship and revere it.

But much like zip-lining in Costa Rica or being front row at a Red Hot Chili Peppers concert, great sex is an incredible life event I know exists. It's just one I've never experienced.

Not that I haven't had sex at all. Far from it. I just haven't had that toe-curling, moan-inducing, leg-shaking kind I've heard so much about. And I have heard about it, because I listen. But all that listening hasn't translated into great sex.

Yet.

And that's not due to lack of enthusiasm on my part. I'd happily enter into a booty boot camp, take a coitus crash course, or study up in a love making masterclass until I've got this thing dialed in once and for all.

But I haven't had the chance.

Which is a head-scratching travesty, but it happens, okay?

Like, if you get involved in a long-term relationship with a woman who's only into sex every other Saturday night, and who only wants missionary, and only with the lights off.

That rule of the bedroom with my ex was, admittedly, bumpy to navigate. Because lights are awesome, what with the way they illuminate the female form and all its curves, dips and delicious valleys.

Also, what the hell was up with the nighttime-only law? I'm sure I'd be super into afternoon delights.

Morning bangs too. My dick certainly seems interested in the a.m.

But hey, I loved her, so I went along with the pencil-in-sex calendar approach.

Twice a month was better than, God forbid, the Gobi Desert of once every four weeks.

Or worse, the vast arctic wasteland of once a year.

My thoughts and prayers go out to all the dudes suffering from birthday-only boinking.

But I know that sex shouldn't be on a schedule. Or if it is, the schedule should be part of the foreplay, like sending dirty daytime texts to your partner about what you're going to do at ten o'clock at night when you finally see each other after a full day of being driven mad with desire.

That kind of planning is the hella sexy kind.

Yay, us.

The next morning, my wife smiles when I wake and tells me she has news.

"What's that, sunshine?"

From her spot in bed, she grabs something from the nightstand and waggles it. A white stick with two pink lines. "Looks like the Stanley Cup winner is going to be a dad."

And yeah, my life keeps getting better. I wrap my arm around her, kiss her like crazy, then slide a hand over her belly.

"Looks like we scored quite a goal."

She kisses me back, smiling for days. "I'd absolutely say we did."

And even though winning the Cup feels awesome, this right here is my real win in life.

THE END

If you missed Dean and Fitz's romance, it's available everywhere in A GUY WALKS INTO MY BAR, an irresistible USA Today Bestseller!

Exciting news, friends! I wrote a sexy romantic comedy with Joe Arden—the popular and award-winning romance narrator who voices many of my heroes in audio! Not only does he have a sexy-as-sin voice, he's funny AF and he can write hot scenes with me! Sweet scenes too! And emotional ones! Our sexy rom-com HOW TO GET LUCKY is coming to you in

And when sex does happen, it shouldn't be in the same position every single time. It should be imaginative.

It should be raw.

And I'm pretty damn sure sex should also be fun.

You know what's *not* fun?

Finding my girlfriend and the dog walker brings new meaning to the phrase *doggie style.*

At least they weren't using a leash.

Why didn't Rex tell me he wasn't getting walked? Poor pooch needed his exercise, and all he was doing was chasing his tail while the ex was giving hers away.

I can't be mad at Rex, though. Not the little dude's fault he was getting stiffed at the same time she was.

But hey, everything happens for a reason, right? I like to believe that anyway.

They say good guys finish last, but I don't believe that. When a good guy finds the right woman, they can both finish. *Together.* A lot.

So, here I am, twenty-eight, single AF, and absolutely ready to find the right woman who'll practice until perfect with me. And then practice some more: every position, kink, and dirty deed.

I'm positive my time has come. That my luck is due for a change. And it feels like I'm holding the winning lottery ticket when a sexy, sweet, sarcastic, brunette walks into my life, and all I can think is yes, yes, yes, it's about fucking time.

Then I learn exactly who she is.

She *is* sexy, sweet, and sarcastic, but she is also . . . *one hundred percent forbidden.*

Which means I'm back to square one.

Until the night she issues me a challenge I can't refuse.

Preorder Preorder How To Get Lucky everywhere!

Sign up for my newsletter to make sure you don't miss a single sexy new book!

ALSO BY LAUREN BLAKELY

FULL PACKAGE, the #1 New York Times Bestselling romantic comedy!

BIG ROCK, the hit New York Times Bestselling standalone romantic comedy!

THE SEXY ONE, a New York Times Bestselling standalone romance!

THE KNOCKED UP PLAN, a multi-week USA Today and Amazon Charts Bestselling standalone romance!

MOST VALUABLE PLAYBOY, a sexy multi-week USA Today Bestselling sports romance! And its companion sports romance, MOST LIKELY TO SCORE!

WANDERLUST, a USA Today Bestselling contemporary romance!

COME AS YOU ARE, a Wall Street Journal and multi-week USA Today Bestselling contemporary romance!

PART-TIME LOVER, a multi-week USA Today Bestselling contemporary romance!

UNBREAK MY HEART, an emotional second chance USA Today Bestselling contemporary romance!

BEST LAID PLANS, a sexy friends-to-lovers USA Today

Bestselling romance!

THE HEARTBREAKERS! The USA Today and WSJ Bestselling rock star series of standalone!

P.S. IT'S ALWAYS BEEN YOU, a sweeping, second chance romance!

A GUY WALKS INTO MY BAR, a sexy, passionate, utterly addictive standalone MM romance!

CONTACT

I love hearing from readers! You can find me on Twitter at LaurenBlakely3, Instagram at LaurenBlakelyBooks, Facebook at LaurenBlakelyBooks, or online at Lauren-Blakely.com. You can also email me at laurenblakely-books@gmail.com

Printed in Great Britain
by Amazon

46788418R00156